Sometimes you have to take what's rightfully yours.

"I'm supposed to trust you?" Harper asked, lowering her voice to a whisper. "When you're trying to steal your best friend's girlfriend?"

All traces of a smirk vanished from Kane's face, and he glared at her with hooded eyes.

"First of all, Grace, I don't believe in trust—which is why I don't believe in best friends. It's easier that way. And second of all, as for stealing his girlfriend . . ."

Harper leaned forward eagerly. She'd been wondering how Kane could justify his scheming, especially when he seemed to have no particular motivation for choosing Beth, of all the girls he could have pursued.

". . . let's just say—karma's a bitch."

"Care to elaborate?" Harper asked.

"No."

SEVEN DEADLY SINS

Lust
Envy

SOON TO BE COMMITTED:
Pride

SEVEN DEADLY SINS

Envy

ROBIN WASSERMAN

SIMON PULSE
New York   London   Toronto   Sydney

ᨃ

SIMON PULSE
An imprint of Simon & Schuster
Children's Publishing Division
1230 Avenue of the Americas, New York, NY 10020
Copyright © 2006 by Robin Wasserman
All rights reserved, including the right of reproduction in whole or in part in any form.
SIMON PULSE and colophon are registered trademarks of Simon & Schuster, Inc.
Designed by Ann Zeak
The text of this book was set in Bembo.
Manufactured in the United States of America
First Simon Pulse edition January 2006
10 9 8 7 6 5 4 3 2 1
Library of Congress Control Number 2005927086
ISBN-13: 978-0-689-87783-4
ISBN-10: 0-689-87783-8

For Grandma

When Envy breeds unkind division:
There comes the ruin, there begins confusion.
—William Shakespeare, *Henry VI, Part I*

You can't always get what you want.
—The Rolling Stones

chapter

1

Beth loved to trace her fingers along the gently curved line of Adam's back. It was her favorite part, this moment, this quiet pause just after they'd finished rolling around beneath the covers (careful not to go too far or to mention the fact that, as always, they stopped just before they did). And just before the inevitable. The tension. The bitter look. The fighting.

No, it was worth it to lie there for a moment, watching the rise and fall of Adam's back as he sprawled on his stomach, spent. Easy to prop herself up and admire his lean, muscled form, to marvel, for the thousandth time, that he was hers, that she was in his bed, that she could lean forward and softly touch her lips to his bare back, that her body still glowed, warm and tingling where he'd last touched her. Better to lie still, breathe deep, enjoy the light streaming through the windows, warming her bare skin, and feel close to him, like their bodies were connected, like they were one. It was always her favorite moment—and it never lasted.

"So, are you still working at the diner tonight?" he asked in a carefully casual tone, stretching and rolling over onto his back.

"Unfortunately." She kissed him again. "You know I'd rather be with you, but . . ."

"I know," he said quickly. Sourly. "Duty calls."

"But maybe I can come over again after school tomorrow?" she asked hopefully. Her voice sounded falsely cheerful, brittle, even to her. But maybe she was imagining that. Maybe he wouldn't notice.

"Can't. Swim meet," he said. "But we're on for Saturday, right?" He sat up in bed and began looking around for his clothes, which had been tossed aside hastily a couple hours before.

"Definitely. Right after that SAT prep meeting." Beth's chest tightened at the thought of it, the test that would define her future. She had only a few weeks left to study, which meant she didn't have the time to waste on a stupid school-sponsored practice test and prep session that would surely fail to teach her anything she didn't already know. But, like all school-sponsored wastes of time, it was mandatory.

"Great," Adam said shortly, pulling a T-shirt over his head. It was pale blue—the same shade as his clear, sparkling eyes.

"Wait!" She sat up and grabbed his wrist, pulling him back to the bed, back to her. She didn't know what to say to him, didn't know how to get back that feeling of closeness that, these days, disappeared every time one of them spoke. It used to be so easy, so comfortable, and now it was like their relationship was some fragile piece of glass. If one of them said the wrong thing, spoke too loudly or too long, it would shatter. So they were careful. They were polite.

They were strangers.

Was it because she'd been so jealous of him and Kaia, the new girl who looked like a model and sounded—to her, at least—like a phone sex operator? Because she had refused to trust him, no matter how many times he'd assured her that nothing, *nothing* would ever happen? Or was it because of what had happened with her and Mr. Powell, the hot French teacher who'd taken such an intense interest in the school newspaper, and an even more intense interest in Beth, its editor in chief? Was it because of the unexpected, unending kiss Powell had suddenly planted on her, a kiss she'd never asked for, that she'd fled from, that she'd said nothing about—but that maybe, deep down, she'd wanted?

Whatever it was, she wanted it to just go away. She wished that she and Adam could somehow find their way back to normal, if only she knew where to start.

"What are you thinking, blue eyes?" he asked, half in and half out of the bed—and his clothes.

She could tell him, and they could talk about it, about everything. Finally, an actual conversation—open, honest, painful. Real. And maybe they could finally try to fix things.

Or not.

"I'm thinking I'm not due at work for another hour," she told him, and threw her arms around his neck, drawing him to her. "I'm thinking that this shirt has got to go."

He obediently pulled it over his head and tossed it back on the floor, then lunged toward her and swept her into his arms. It wasn't open or honest, and it wouldn't fix anything. But it was easy. And right now, easy was all she could handle.

In most towns the Nifty Fifties Diner, with its rancid burgers, temperamental jukebox, tacky decor, and rude waitresses, would have quickly become an empty shell, housing a few lonely patrons whose taste buds had long since abandoned them. Empty on weekends, scorned by the breakfast crew, it would, by all rights, have lasted about six months before the owners shut its doors and got the hell out of town. But this wasn't most towns. This was Grace, California, where haute cuisine meant ordering from the booth rather than at the counter, and even MacDonald's feared to tread. In Grace you took what you could get, and pretty much all you could get was the Nifty Fifties Diner, wilted French fries, surly service, and all.

Which is why every day after school, a crowd of bored teens crowded its way into the diner's rusty orange booths. But it wasn't just the desperation that drove them to it. Harper Grace (formerly of Grace Mines; Grace Library; Grace, California—currently of Grace Dry Cleaning on Fourth and Main) had been known to favor the place with her presence. And after all, the masses concluded, if Harper Grace and her crew deigned to eat there, it must have some redeeming quality.

As far as Harper was concerned, it had one and only one: It was there.

Actually, make that two, she thought, snagging a fry off

Miranda's plate. As usual, her best friend had eaten about one-tenth of her order and spent the past hour pushing the rest of the food around on her plate.

One: The diner was there.

Two: Everyone in it cared less about the food than about watching Harper's every move. It was just like school . . . only without all the boring parts. Popularity without the homework.

And she so loved the attention.

"Think Beth is working today?" Miranda asked, looking around for the blond bombshell they both loved to hate.

"Who knows?" Harper asked, rolling her eyes. "Who cares?"

Miranda laughed. "Be nice, Harper," she warned, but Harper knew she didn't really mean it. For one thing, Harper Grace hadn't clawed her way up the school's social ladder by being nice. For another, rule number one of their friendship was that Harper said aloud all the bitchy thoughts Miranda was too polite to voice. Why mess with tradition?

"What, would you prefer she be here hovering over us with that stupid smile?" Harper gave Miranda her best Beth Manning grin and affected a high and fluttery voice. "'Hey guys! Can I get you anything? Water? Coffee? My backbone? Don't worry, I won't be needing it.'"

"You're right," Miranda admitted with a sly smile. "Much better she be off somewhere with Adam. Better making out with him than bothering us."

And at that, all traces of joy vanished from Harper's face.

"I'm eating here, Rand," she complained. "Can we keep the vomit-inducing comments to a minimum?"

Miranda shook her head in apology. "I'm sorry, it just slipped out. I'm a little off today."

"Yeah, what's the deal with that, Rand? I know why *I'm* climbing the walls," Harper whined, the image of a blissful Beth and Adam popping, unbidden, into her head. There had been a moment, back at the beginning of the school year, when she'd thought she had a chance. Especially when, in a moment of weakness, Adam had turned his back on true love—and slept with someone else. Just two little problems with that scenario. First, the "someone else" wasn't Harper. Second, Beth had no idea that her perfect boyfriend had cheated on her. The golden couple was still going strong, and Harper was still out in the cold.

She noticed everything, every look, every touch that passed between Adam and the girl he thought he loved. Every day, it seemed, Harper was treated to an endless series of disgusting displays, her days at school transformed into a constant reminder of what she wanted and couldn't have. And, since Adam lived next door, his bedroom window facing hers, her nights weren't much of an improvement. Needless to say, these days she was a little off her game.

"Yeah, I know why my life sucks," Harper said bitterly. "What's wrong with yours?"

"I can't stop thinking about him," Miranda admitted.

"Kane?" Harper's heart sank. Miranda hadn't mentioned the local lothario in days, and Harper had hoped that this little chapter was over. No such luck, apparently.

"I know, I know, he's out of my league," Miranda complained.

"No, you know that's not true," Harper assured her. But it was a halfhearted protest. Kane Geary was handsome, cocky, a consummate asshole—and had privately confirmed for Harper that the Miranda thing was a no go. He had his sights set on someone else. It hadn't come as a huge surprise. Miranda was many things—smart, caustic, funny, and at least a seven or eight on the ten point scale—but she wasn't some gorgeous bimbo who would strip down to her thong in a wink of Kane's eye. And as far as Kane was concerned, that pretty much took her out of the running.

"No, it's true. He's out of my league," Miranda insisted. "But I've been thinking." She grinned, and her voice took on the same "can do" bravado it had had back in fifth grade when she'd convinced Harper they should start their very own babysitter's club. Harper issued a silent groan. That plan hadn't worked either.

"It's time for a New Miranda Stevens," she continued. (Harper could hear the capital N in her voice.)

"Uh, do I get a vote?" Harper asked, raising her hand in protest. "Because I like the old Miranda."

"Are you six feet tall with dark brown eyes, washboard abs, and a killer smile?"

Harper rolled her eyes.

"Then no," Miranda confirmed. "You don't get a vote. So here's what I'm thinking. . . ."

Harper sighed as Miranda began to outline a self-improvement strategy that included hair, makeup, fashion, body, and personality makeovers, and so much detail Harper was surprised it wasn't accompanied by a PowerPoint presentation. Was she supposed to tell her best friend to give it up, that Kane would never be interested in her? Or that the "someone else" Kane was after was Beth? Was she supposed to admit that she'd secretly agreed to help Kane get Beth, if he would help her get Adam? Should she tell her best friend in the world that she'd basically screwed her over and made a pact with the devil, that all was fair in love and war, and Miranda would just have to deal?

Yeah, that would go over really well.

"So, are you in?" Miranda asked.

"What?" Harper could tell by the self-satisfied grin on Miranda's face that while she'd been zoned out in guilt land, the lengthy presentation had finally come to a close.

"Will you help? With the New Miranda?"

"I told you, I kind of like the old one," Harper hedged.

"Harper! Have you been listening to anything I've said? I need to do this if I'm ever going to get Kane to notice me—and you *swore* you'd help me get together with him."

"I remember," Harper said. And she did. The promise echoed in her ears every time she saw Miranda, and it faded just as quickly every time she saw Beth wrap her tentacles around Adam. She needed Kane's help on this one—more, apparently, than she needed Miranda's trust.

Though maybe if she played things right, she could get both.

"Besides," Miranda wheedled, "you're my best friend. This is what you're here for. If I can't count on you, who can I count on?"

Good question.

✧✧✧

"Where are we going?" Heather giggled. At least, he thought her name was Heather.

"Shh. I told you, it's a surprise!" Kane whispered as they crept down the empty halls of the high school, deserted now that the last of the after school meetings had disbanded and all the teachers had climbed into their dismal cars and driven home to their dismal lives. Kane supposed that there were those who wouldn't see the point of sneaking *into* school—but some people just didn't have any vision.

"What if we get caught?" Heather whispered.

Kane grinned and gave her a quick peck on the lips. It was a sexy whisper, nothing like the shrill screeching that passed for her regular voice. She had an amazing body, a passable face, but that voice—it could make your ears bleed. Kane suspected that after today's little adventure, it would be time to show Heather the door. Unless he wanted to make illegal trespassing a constant theme of their dating life. Which, come to think of it, had some possibility. . . .

"We won't get caught," he promised her. "And if we do, I'll take all the blame."

She giggled again. "My hero."

They stopped abruptly in front of an unmarked door and Kane pulled out a key similar to the one he'd used to get them into the building.

"Where did you—?"

He put a finger to her lips, then silenced her with another kiss.

"The master never reveals his secrets," he explained.

"Don't ask—just enjoy." He pushed open the doors and ushered her down the stairs to the dark and deserted boiler room. Heather clung to him in fear and admiration as he made his way around the room by memory, setting up the candles and mohair blanket he'd brought along.

"Voilà!" he finally said in triumph. Soft candlelight lit up the room. It was a romantic getaway, of sorts—and it was clearly enough for Heather.

For all the Heathers of the world, Kane thought. It always was. And he was getting a little tired of it. He'd always looked down on the guys at school with steady girlfriends, *relationships.* Suckers, he'd thought. Tying themselves down to one girl, being responsible, being trapped, and for what? A guaranteed date on Valentine's Day? A constant ego boost? A steady source of blow jobs?

Kane had all that already. And without all the whining, complaining, and demanding that seemed to come along with having a girlfriend.

On the other hand, lately, when he looked at Adam and Beth together, when he saw the way she looked at him, held him, Kane wondered. Was he missing out? Was it possible that Adam had stumbled onto something better? Kane didn't believe there was anything out there better than the life he'd crafted for himself. But he had to be sure, because if there was, he would do whatever was in his power to have it.

In the meantime he'd have no trouble finding something, or someone, to occupy his time. . . .

Heather wrapped her body around him, running her fingers through his hair.

"You're amazing," she whispered, kissing his ear, his neck, his chest.

Kane let her pull his shirt over his head and watched in appreciation as her pert breasts, tucked into a red satin bra, made an appearance, accompanied by a tan, taut stomach and slender, perfect legs. Then she pressed against him again, her hands massaging their way down his back—and he had other things to appreciate.

"You're totally amazing," she repeated.

"Yeah—I know."

Kaia took a long sip of her vodka tonic and stretched out along the shallow bench of the Jacuzzi, her long, jet black hair fanned out along the marble edge. She closed her eyes and moaned in appreciation as the jets pummeled her muscles and all of her stress melted away into the steaming water.

Not that she had much to be stressed about. Stress required caring what happened, wanting something, worrying about something, *doing* something—and none of that posed much of a problem in the lame exercise in small town boredom that passed for her life these days. No, any stress she'd had was left behind in New York, along with her friends, her boyfriends, her uncaring bitch of a mother, and her Saks Fifth Avenue credit card. All this apathy was probably doing wonders for her complexion—too bad there was no one around to see.

"Need a refill, Ms. Sellers?" the maid asked cautiously.

"No thanks, Alicia," Kaia said sweetly. It was useful to be nice—sometimes—to the help. After all, she didn't think her father—if he ever came back from his latest business trip—would appreciate hearing that she'd drunk her way through half his liquor cabinet. Right now it was her and Alicia's little secret, and Kaia intended it to stay that way.

It was a good thing, too, because if it weren't for the Jacuzzi and the booze, and the satellite TV, she'd go crazy out here.

Ever since her mother had shipped her out to the middle of nowhere, claiming that a year at her father's house in the desert would do wonders for her character, life had become one long, uninterrupted stretch of tedium. While her mother was taking full advantage of her new childless state, whoring around New York's spas, sales, and singles bars like a middle-aged Hilton sister, Kaia was stuck here in this scorching hot ghost town, making nice with the low-rent losers who made up the local teen scene. She'd caught only the occasional glimpse of her father, who'd claimed he was delighted to have her, then promptly left town, returning to his desert McMansion and his delinquent daughter for a few hours each week before getting the hell out again.

Kaia couldn't blame him. If she had the cash, she'd head for the hills (or better, L.A., only a six-hour drive away) and never look back.

But Daddy Dearest had sliced through all her credit cards, so she was stuck. Now that she'd proven to herself that she could bed the two hottest guys in school—and for such a small and pathetic school, they were pretty damn hot—she was fresh out of ideas. Adam Morgan, with all of his supposed virtue and loyalty, hadn't been much of a challenge, but the payoff had been fun, though not as much fun as watching his puppy dog face crumble when she'd blown him off a heartbeat later. Kane, on the other hand, had been no challenge at all, but that's not to say he didn't have his merits. . . .

But now it was only October, and she was already bored. Again. What next? Storm the "popular crowd" and get voted homecoming queen? Rededicate herself to last month's quest of screwing—and then screwing over—the dashing French teacher who seemed to think he was too good for her? Snag one of her father's credit cards and get the hell back to New York?

Kaia let her head sink under the water for a moment and then burst back above the surface, the cool desert air stinging her dripping face. She was too blissfully comfortable right now to worry about tomorrow, or the next day. She was sure that eventually she'd manage to find herself some interesting trouble.

She always did.

Adam brushed Beth's blond hair out of her face and gave her a soft kiss on the forehead. This time when he climbed out of bed and began to hunt around for his clothes, she made no move to pull him back down. It was too bad; things were so much easier when they were kissing instead of talking.

Then he didn't have to worry about all the things he wasn't allowed to say, things that kept threatening to spill from his lips. Things like, say, "I slept with Kaia." Every time he opened his mouth, he feared the confession would pop out. Part of him just wanted it out in the open. Anything to be free of all this crushing guilt.

And, of course, when they were in the midst of hooking up, they were also relieved of the burden of not talking about the reason they always *stopped* hooking up. It was the only time they could, for once, ignore their biggest problem: sex—or the lack thereof.

It had been bad enough this summer, when it seemed like he couldn't say anything right, when Beth assumed sex was all he wanted and seemed to silently hate him for it. Almost as much as he hated himself . . . because sometimes it felt like sex *was* all he wanted. But ever since the dance at the beginning of the school year, things had, on the surface, been much better—and beneath the surface, where it counted, much, much worse.

It was all a little hazy for him, but from what he could piece together from his drunken, fragmented memory of the night, Beth had decided that she was ready to sleep with him—and he'd passed out. When he awoke, sometime early the next morning, she was staring at him in disgust and wouldn't say a word.

They hadn't talked about it then, or the next day, or any time afterward. She had never brought it up. And he had never apologized.

And now sex, such a hot topic before, was off limits. Taboo. He never asked what had happened to her being "ready," or when she might be again. Certainly never mentioned that he now knew what sex was like—and how much he wanted more of it. Sometimes he envied Kane, who could get any girl he wanted and could get anything out of her. Not that he would ever give up what he had with Beth, but sometimes he wished he could just take a break. Slip into a parallel universe where he was single. Free.

"So, it's looking like the swim team might make it to the championships this year," he said, trying to wipe such thoughts from his mind and searching for a neutral subject. Making it work with Beth meant *not* dwelling on what he couldn't have. What he shouldn't even want. "We're having a pretty strong season."

"I know," she said with a rueful smile. "I wish I could make it to your meet tomorrow."

"It's okay," he assured her, looking away. "I know you're busy." Last year Beth had come to all of his swim meets and basketball games, and cheered him on from the sidelines. This year she'd been too busy to make it to any of them. And he'd tried to pretend he didn't care.

"If we do make it to the championships," he began tentatively, "I think a bunch of kids from school will probably come along, sort of a cheering section, and maybe—"

"I'd love to go!" Beth cried. She hopped out of bed and gave him a quick hug before pulling on her denim skirt and a light pink tank top. "I mean, if you want me to be there. . . ."

"Of course I do," he said hastily, giving her a soft kiss. "I've missed my good luck charm. And it'd be fun to be there together. Good for . . . us, you know?"

"Speaking of us, Adam, I think we should—well, we haven't really . . ." Her voice trailed off.

"What?" he prompted her gently, not really sure he wanted to hear the answer.

"Uh, I just think I should get going," she said, her voice suddenly brisk and cheerful. "I want to get in some studying before work."

"You have a test tomorrow?" It seemed unlikely. Usually when there was a test imminent, he knew it. It was generally pretty hard to miss—Beth had flashcards, study sessions, not to mention an endless litany of concerns about failing out of school—culminating, each time, in the inevitable A.

"No, for the SATs—you know, life-altering event only a few weeks away?" she reminded him.

"Plenty of time for that later," he scoffed, pulling her toward him. She pushed him away. Sometimes their relationship felt like an endless tug of war. He pulled her in one direction, and something within her kept pulling in the other.

"This is my future—*our* future—that we're talking about here," she said passionately. "It's *important*."

"I know, I know," he said, trying to reassure her.

"You are coming on Saturday, right?" she asked, suddenly suspicious. "You know this thing is mandatory, right?"

"I know, you don't have to remind me a million times," he complained, turning away from her. "I'm not an idiot."

"I just wish you'd take these things a little more seriously," she whined. "You're always—"

"What?" He tensed. Along with sex, they usually tried not to discuss the future—neither wanted to acknowledge that they were headed in two very different directions.

"Nothing." She came up behind him and put her arms around him, massaging his chest and kissing his neck. "Let's just forget it," she mumbled, her lips against his skin.

It worked for him.

It was the worst possible timing.

Harper pulled into the driveway, and there they were, a few yards away, wrapped in each other's arms. Couldn't they ever just give it a rest?

"Hey, Harper!" Adam called to her in his lilting Southern accent. It was the one thing he'd held on to from an early childhood in South Carolina. Adam hated it, as he hated any reminder of his distant past. But to Harper, his voice was like a song, sweet and intoxicating. "Come over and say hello!"

"Can't, busy, gotta—you know," she babbled, waving back as she raced for her front door.

Awkward postcoital convo with the love of her life and the love of his? No thanks.

Besides, they'd already forgotten her existence and gotten back to the serious business of groping each other. Harper shook her head in disgust and slammed through the doorway. When Adam had confessed to Harper—his oldest and most trustworthy friend—that he'd cheated on Beth, Harper had been sure that their relationship wouldn't last the week. But the incident had proved nothing more than a hiccup, a tiny bump in the path of disgustingly true love. In fact, if their nonstop PDAs were any indication, he and Beth were going stronger than ever. It killed Harper to know that, with a few carefully chosen words, she could destroy their happiness. She could drive Beth away—but Adam would never forgive her.

Ignorance is bliss, Beth—right?

As for Adam, he'd never mentioned Kaia after that, and now, once again, all he could talk about was his perfect, wonderful Beth.

Screw that. Harper was done waiting around for Adam to wake up and discover he was with the wrong girl. Harper the passive good girl (if she'd ever existed) was gone. Harper the scheming bitch was back in action.

And finally, she had the beginnings of an idea. . . .

chapter

2

Saturday morning, Haven High, room 232. The disgruntled seniors, all forty-eight of them, filtered into the room, spitting out variations on the same theme.

It was Saturday.

It was early.

And in a just world, they would all be at home in bed.

No one wanted to be there.

Not Kane, bleary-eyed and hungover from last night's revelry, who thought studying was for saps and that SAT prep courses, even the lame one-time freebie offered by their tiny public school, should be reserved for those too stupid to score well on their own.

Not Adam, who'd decided he didn't need the SATs or college—not when he was planning to stay in Grace until the day he died.

Not Beth, for whom every minute wasted in the classroom listening to the teacher drone on was a minute she wasn't able to spend shut up in her room poring over Princeton Review books and searching for the magic strategy that would guarantee her a perfect score. (And the fact that the class was led by Mr. Powell, that she could feel his eyes boring into her even as she stared resolutely down at her desk? It didn't help.)

And certainly not Jack Powell, who, as the newest hire, had been compelled to "volunteer" for the Saturday class. Sacrifice his morning. Stare down Beth and pray she wouldn't grow a spine (or a mouth). Avoid the penetrating gaze of Kaia, whose very unwelcome and very public liplock with him in the middle of a school dance had left him the focus of hallway gossip, faculty lounge whispering, strict administrative scrutiny—and temporary probation.

No, Jack Powell would rather be at home and in bed too. Jack Powell would, in fact, rather be strapped into a dentist's chair getting a root canal.

But no one had asked him.

"Okay kids, quiet down," he called out in his clipped British accent. He was only too aware of its charm—he'd made girls swoon all up and down the eastern seaboard, and it wasn't surprising that the upper crust London inflection had an even greater effect out in this desert wasteland. "I know you don't want to be here."

Shouts of agreement.

Join the club, he thought, with more than a trace of bitterness. If his former colleagues could see him now, stranded in the middle of nowhere, policing these deadbeats-in-training. None of them knew how good they had it. He hadn't known himself, until he'd ended up in this godforsaken corner of the world. And the worst part was, he had no one to blame but himself.

"Well, let's make it quick and painless, then." He began to distribute a practice test—at least that would keep them busy for an hour or so.

He looked around at the roomful of students with a flicker of pity. *They don't pay me enough to work on Saturdays,* he reminded himself, *but hell, these suckers have to be here for nothing.*

Two hours later Beth staggered out of the school, feeling like she'd just emerged, not entirely unscathed, from an emotional car wreck. Sitting through French class with Powell was bad enough. Especially with the whole school buzzing about Kaia's kiss at the dance: Debate still raged as to whether Kaia had thrown herself at the clueless young teacher—or whether the dashing Jack Powell was, in fact, carrying on a not-so-secret affair with his hottest student and God knew who else. Beth flushed every time the subject came up and just hoped no one could read the truth that was, she feared, written all over her red cheeks and tortured frown.

She still couldn't believe that she'd been stupid enough to trust him. Yes, he was the new sponsor of the newspaper and she was its editor in chief—at the time it had made sense that he'd want to spend a series of long, intimate afternoons together, going over logistics—but it had been more than that, right from the start, hadn't it? "Call me Jack," he'd suggested—she shuddered at the memory. She had trusted him, believed in him, confided in him, until that final day. When it turned out that all he wanted was—

"Beth, wake up!"

That was the trouble with zoning out—it made it a lot harder to avoid the people you didn't want to see. People like Harper Grace. Haven High's resident alpha girl: best dressed, best coiffed, best bitch. And, oh yeah, Adam's best friend.

"Hey, Harper," Beth greeted her, hoping her grin didn't seem too fake.

She didn't like Harper, didn't trust Harper—but since she'd drifted away from her real girlfriends a few months into the relationship with Adam, she also didn't have too many other options.

Harper pulled her away from the crowd of students milling across the school grounds and gave her a conspiratorial grin.

"So, I've been meaning to ask you," she said softly. "How are things going with you and Adam?"

"Uh . . . okay," Beth responded guardedly.

"No," Harper leaned in even closer. "I mean with, you know, that *problem* you were having."

"I'm not sure what you mean." But Beth had a sinking feeling that she did. She'd made the mistake of confessing her fears about sex, and about her relationship, to Harper. The conversation hadn't been a total nightmare, but she wasn't looking for an instant replay anytime soon.

"I've been so concerned about you," Harper said, linking her arm through Beth's. "I mean, I just feel so terrible for you, with all your issues."

Beth pulled her arm away but forced herself to do it with a smile. Adam was always urging her to see the good in Harper, and so for his sake she'd tried, and failed, and tried again. She was still working on it—the least she could do in the meantime was be polite.

"So . . . you two still haven't . . . ?" Harper prodded.

"That's really none of your business," Beth snapped.

Harper looked at her appraisingly. Beth squirmed under the scrutiny of her gaze.

"Mmm-hmm, that's what I thought," Harper said finally, nodding her head.

"Look, I really have to go," Beth told her, pulling away, wishing that a hole would open up and swallow her before their little chat could go any further.

"No, no, I almost forgot why I wanted to talk to you in the first place," Harper said, once again threading her arm through Beth's as if they were the best of friends. As if they were anything. "So, listen, you aced that practice test, right?"

Beth darted her eyes toward the ground and reddened slightly.

"I guess. . . . Why?"

"We knew it!" Harper said triumphantly.

"We?"

"Me—and Kane. Look, he'd kill me if he knew I was telling you this, but Kane's not too hot on standardized tests. He's a smart guy, but he just freezes up. Have you heard that rumor, how they give you six hundred points just for writing your name?"

"Uh-huh," she mumbled dubiously.

"Well, let's just say Kane's going to need it."

Beth snuck a glance over at the Greek god of Haven High, preening for a couple of blondes from the cheerleading team. Beth wasn't surprised to hear he was lagging behind. From what she'd seen of Kane (another one of Adam's friends whose "good side" was impossibly difficult to find), his definition of a hard day's work involved vodka, girls, and plenty of naps. Still, it didn't seem like her business—or her problem.

"Why are you telling me this, Harper?" she asked, again pulling her arm away.

"Kane doesn't want to be stuck in this deadbeat town any more than the rest of us," Harper explained. "Which means college. Which means decent SAT scores. Which means . . . he needs your help."

"Me?" Beth wrinkled her face in surprise—but a warm rush of pride began to spread through her. That they were desperate, and they'd come to her, needed her . . .

"You," Harper confirmed. "He wants you to tutor him."

"Then why isn't he asking me himself?"

Harper laughed and shrugged. "You know guys, they're idiots. He's just embarrassed. Kane can be a little shy sometimes, you know?"

"Kane?" Beth repeated in disbelief. She looked back toward the entrance of the school, where Kane had hoisted one of the cheerleaders into his arms and was now spinning her around as she squealed in mock dismay. He didn't look shy to her. Arrogant, maybe. Sleazy. Impressed with his own existence. All of the above. But shy?

"I'm not really going to have that much time," she cautioned Harper. "I don't know if—"

"Beth, he *needs* you," Harper pleaded. "Really, you're his only hope. He told me he knew you were the only one who'd be able to help him."

"Really?" When she was eleven, Beth had found a three-legged jackrabbit lying in her backyard and, with her father's help, had nursed it back to health. She'd never been able to say no to desperation—and today was no different. "Well, I guess if he needs me . . ."

"Great!" Harper tore a piece of paper from her notebook and scrawled something on it before handing it to Beth. "Here's his number. I'll tell him you're going to call ASAP."

And she skipped away before Beth had a chance to change her mind.

Mission accomplished—and so easily that it was difficult to feel too proud of herself.

But Harper managed.

"You are going to love me," she crowed into her cell once Kane answered the phone.

"Not unless you're waiting for me in the parking lot with some black coffee and a Playboy bunny," Kane retorted. "Otherwise, I'm kind of busy right now."

"Yeah, I can see that." Harper, about a hundred yards away, sneered at the sight of his adoring harem. Had these girls no respect for themselves?

Stupid question.

"What do you mean, you can see?" Kane looked up from the nearest buxom brunette and began scanning the parking lot.

"On your left, loser boy." Harper waved lazily until he spotted her. "And you're not too busy for this. Trust me."

She snapped the phone shut and watched as Kane grudgingly kissed the girls good-bye and jogged over.

"This better be good," he grumbled once he'd reached her. "I've been bored long enough for one day. I need to go out and wash off the stench of all this educational earnestness with some good, old-fashioned debauchery."

"What you need is to go home and study for the SATs," Harper countered.

"The SATs?" he asked incredulously.

She nodded.

"The SATs that are three weeks away?"

She nodded again.

"The SATs that I couldn't give a shit about?"

"You got it."

"Harper, you know that practice test in there? I scored above a seven hundred on every section. You know what that means?" He spoke slowly and patiently, as if she would soon be taking her own test—English as a second language. "It means I'm not studying today, tomorrow—hell, I may never study again."

Harper gave him a gentle pat on the back and shook her head sadly. "No, you're going home and cracking the books. Right now, and tomorrow, and the next day. You're going to make the library your new best friend."

"And why would I want to do that?" he sneered.

Harper grinned, and jerked a thumb across the parking lot toward Beth, who was climbing into Adam's rusty maroon Chevrolet.

"Meet your new tutor."

Kane's eyes widened. "You didn't!"

"Oh, I did."

Harper laid out her vision for him—long, late nights huddled together over the books; frequent breaks for coffee, pizza, and intimate getting-to-know-you sessions; close quarters; moonlit strolls; high stress, low inhibitions—when Harper Grace made a deal, she delivered. And even Kane had to admit that she had just delivered Beth to his doorstep, complete with gift wrap and ruffled bow.

"And while I'm sweeping Beth off her feet with my charm and feigned stupidity, I assume you'll be . . . taking care of Adam?"

Harper allowed herself a moment to enjoy a second vision: Adam, sitting at home, bored, lonely, angry, jealous, and primed for . . . well, anything.

"A girl's gotta do what a girl's gotta do," she said sweetly.

Kane laughed and slung an arm around her shoulders.

"And I have no doubt, Grace," he assured her, "that you're just the girl to do it."

Having finished eavesdropping on the pathetic scheming out in the parking lot, Kaia headed back inside the school to take care of some unfinished business. Watching Harper and Kane haplessly put together their juvenile little plot had inspired her—why should they be the only ones having any fun?

She tugged down her silk tank top and hitched up her blue miniskirt so that her perfect (and worth every cent) cleavage and Pilates-sculpted thighs had maximum visibility. Then she stepped inside the classroom. Jack Powell may have thought he could avoid her forever, but his time had just run out.

"Hey, Mr. Powell," she whispered, leaning against the door frame and aiming an unmistakable look in his direction, familiar to any adult-movie fan as a silent "Hey, big guy, throw me down and do me right here on the floor" invitation. It was intended to be ironic. Partly. "Long time, no see."

"I see you every day in class, Ms. Sellers," he said. She shivered at the sound of his voice. "And trust me, that's quite enough."

He turned his back on her. Big mistake.

Kaia closed the door and crossed the empty classroom, shedding the cheesy sex-me-up grin as she went. It seemed Mr. Powell was still playing hard to get—and she was beginning to enjoy his game. She laid a light hand on the small of his back, saying, "I see *you* every day in French— but I'm not sure you're really seeing me."

He whirled around to face her and backed away.

"What kind of game are you playing?" he hissed. "Isn't it enough for you that I'm on probation after your little stunt at the dance? It was all I could do to talk them out of firing me."

"Hey, don't look at me, I'm the victim here," Kaia countered. "According to Mr. Hemp, at least." Kaia had been reprimanded for her "flagrant disregard of Mr. Powell's personal space" and had been sentenced to six weeks' worth of meetings with the school psychologist, who, she suspected, had received his pseudo degree off the Internet, if not purchased it at Shrinks "R" Us. She would have preferred a prison term.

"Victim?" He snorted. "I'm warning you, Kaia, if you're trying to spread some kind of—if you think you can set me up—"

"Chill out, Jack." She flashed an insouciant grin. "I

think you got my message. This time I come in peace. I want to call a truce."

"A truce?" he repeated dubiously. "So this means you're going to stop throwing yourself at me and end this apparent quest to get me fired?"

"Provisional yes to the latter, definite no to the former." She leaned forward to give him a quick peck on the lips, but he twisted his face away, and instead her lips brushed his coarse stubble. Good enough. "You want me, Mr. Powell. You just don't know it yet. But you will."

"I want you to get out of here," he said coldly, "and make sure that no one sees you go. And then I want you to drop French and do me the favor of pretending I don't exist. Or at least letting me pretend that about you. Let's start now."

He sat down at the desk and began shuffling through a stack of papers, pointedly refusing to look at her.

Kaia stood before him, hands on her hips, shaking her head and clucking her tongue against the roof of her mouth, like a mother reprimanding her young.

"Mr. Powell, I thought we'd already established that if I want to, I can make life here very unpleasant for you. You said it yourself—I can be trouble. You're right. I don't think you want to be rude to me."

Silence. And more paper shuffling.

"Okay," Kaia agreed, heading for the door. "You're lucky I'm in a 'make love, not war' mood . . . for now."

After escaping the SAT session, Beth and Adam treated themselves to an impromptu picnic in Dwyer Park (complete with brownish tufts of grass, brownish decaying picket fence, and brownish pond—as desert oases went, it ranked somewhere between Palm Springs and a garbage dump). Once they'd gotten everything set up, Adam ran off to grab them some soda from the nearby drugstore. Beth's phone rang as soon as he was gone.

It was Kane. She'd left a message for him just after leaving the school, so she wasn't surprised to see his name pop up on her caller ID. Still, it was strange—he'd never called her before. And if he had, she probably wouldn't have picked up the phone.

They only spoke for a few minutes, just enough time to agree on the tutoring and pick a time for their first meeting. But the conversation wasn't nearly as awkward as she'd feared—and weirdly, Beth found herself almost looking forward to their first encounter.

She put the phone away with a quizzical frown. Kane had seemed so genuine, so earnest, so pleasant, so . . . totally un-Kane-like. He'd limited himself to only two sarcastic comments and one sexual innuendo. For a five-minute conversation, it had to be a personal best. And even stranger—he actually seemed to want her help. He seemed to want to do well, whatever it would take.

Kane? Working? Had she walked out of the school this morning and into some alternate universe?

The Kane she knew—though, granted, she didn't know him very well and had never wanted to change that—thought hard work meant applying a little extra torque when opening a stuck bottle lid. And even that was only worth it if the bottle contained some kind of alcoholic beverage or was handed to him by a weak and soon to be very grateful cheerleader. Back before she and Adam had gotten together, Kane had chased after her, as he did every girl—for about a day. She'd blown him off, and he'd disappeared. Kane didn't believe in making an effort.

She shook her head. This time he really must be desperate.

"Who was on the phone?" Adam asked, sitting down on the worn quilt that served as their picnic blanket and passing her a deliciously cool bottle of Coke.

"Your best friend, actually." Searching for a relief from the searing, dry heat of the afternoon, she pressed the bottle against her forehead, enjoying the icy chill that ran down her spine.

"Harper?" he asked, confused.

Beth flinched. She respected Adam's friendship with the beautiful girl next door, but she didn't have to like it.

"No, your other best friend—you remember Kane, don't you?"

Adam shook his head in disgust. "What, is he trying to track me down? Dude, I never should have told him I was going out with you today."

"Actually, he was looking for me," Beth said, smacking him lightly with an annoyance that was only half for show.

"You? Why would he be calling you?"

"People have been known to want to talk to me," she informed him, irritation mounting.

"I know, I know," Adam murmured, kissing her on the forehead. "You're in high demand. In fact," he added, kissing his way down her nose and landing on her lips, "I want you right now."

"He wants my help," Beth explained, somewhat mollified. "With studying for the SATs."

"Kane? Studying?" Adam burst into laughter. "I don't think so. Seriously, what did he want?"

"I know, I thought it was weird too," Beth admitted. "But he seems to really want a tutor."

"And he asked *you*?"

"Why wouldn't he ask me?"

"I just meant—whatever," Adam stopped himself. "So he's had a personality overhaul and wants a tutor for the SATs. You're not going to do it, are you?"

"Of course I am—he's my friend," she reminded him. "Well . . . he's your friend. And he needs my help. Why wouldn't I do it?"

"Oh, I don't know, maybe because these days you're too busy to eat or sleep, not to mention see your boyfriend?" He kept his voice level and light, but Beth could feel the dangerous tension bubbling beneath the surface. There just didn't seem to be much she could do about it—and she couldn't stop herself from egging him on.

"Not all of us want to spend our lives lying around watching TV and drinking beer," she snapped, hating herself for it the moment she heard the words slip out of her mouth. "At least Kane cares about something and is willing to work hard to get it. How could I say no to that?"

"Fine," he grunted.

"Fine." And, after a moment, "we're starting tomorrow."

"What?" he yelped. "We've got plans for tomorrow!"

"I know," she said in a gentler voice. "I'm sorry—it's just, he wanted to get started right away, and he seemed so desperate . . ."

"You see? This is exactly what I'm talking about! How

hard was it to find some time together this weekend, and now you're just . . . ?" He threw up his arms in disgust.

"Adam, stop." Beth took his hands in hers and clasped them to his chest. "I'm here, with you, now. Can't we just enjoy this?"

He didn't respond, but he left his hands in hers, and she felt a gentle pressure squeezing back. Beth looked around—the park was mostly empty, and they were partially hidden from view by a cluster of decrepit trees.

She brought his hands to her lips and kissed them softly, then released them. He grazed his fingers across her cheekbones and cradled her face.

"How about if we stop talking about Kane for a while?" she suggested, lying back on the quilt and pulling him down beside her. He stroked her hair, and she breathed in the nearness of him, the familiar scent that somehow evoked both a cozy kitchen of fresh baked bread and the wide expanse of a bright summer morning. "Why don't we just—"

"Stop talking *at all* for a while?" he finished for her, his hands slipping under her pale pink shirt and massaging her bare skin.

Beth sighed, feeling her tension slip away. It sounded like a plan.

chapter

3

"How about this?" Miranda crept out of the dressing room and timidly spun around to display the newest ensemble— bright red capri pants that looked like they'd been painted on, paired with a black lace corset whose tackiness quotient would have made Christina Aguilera cringe.

Uh, no.

Harper sighed. Three hours into the total transformation shopping trip (step one on the road to a new and improved Miranda, whatever that was supposed to mean) and she was bored out of her mind. Shopping in Grace was never the most thrilling of experiences since the options consisted of three or four sorry stores in a local excuse for a strip mall, a large thrift shop (useless, since the middle-aged Grace matrons who made up its pool of suppliers couldn't really be counted on to supply the type of "vintage" threads recommended in last month's *Vogue*), and, of course, the Wal-Mart out on Route 53 (the less said about that, the better).

No, Harper preferred to buy most of her clothes online—and Harper's parents preferred her not to buy clothes at all, as the meager profits from the family dry cleaning business rarely seemed to justify that kind of supposedly wasteful expenditure. Harper failed to see how a fur-lined J Crew raincoat or tan suede boots could be deemed wasteful—so what if the temperature never dipped below sixty degrees and it rained only eight inches a year? Sometimes fashion was its own excuse. Regardless, Harper had managed—just barely—to put together a wardrobe befitting her position in Haven High's social strata. It didn't mean that she wanted to spend a Sunday afternoon watching Miranda fork over daddy's credit card in return for an armful of clothes she didn't need and would never wear—*especially* when phase one of Operation Anti-Cupid was in full effect and Adam was, even now, sitting home alone, ripe for the picking.

But Harper was still feeling nagging guilt about helping the love of Miranda's life pursue someone else. So here she was, figuring the least she could do was save her ever faithful sidekick from making a serious fashion faux pas.

After all, what are friends for?

"Well . . . I suppose Halloween is coming up," Harper finally said, and gave her a thumbs down.

Miranda studied herself in the mirror from a number of angles before wrinkling her nose and sighing. "You're right, as usual." She disappeared back inside the dressing room. "Just a couple more things," she called out.

Harper checked her watch and then leaned back against the wall, pressing her weight against it as she slumped to the floor. Was this going to drag on forever?

"What about this?" Miranda asked, popping out of the dressing room, a hesitant smile creeping across her face. She had slipped into a snugly fitting suede skirt, paired with a gauzy green shirt that laced up the front, offering a glimpse of cleavage and leaving just enough to the imagination.

It was stylish, edgy, slightly daring—it was, in other words, totally Harper.

It looked okay on Miranda, Harper judged, but she could almost feel that suede wrapping around her legs and knew that shade of green would light her auburn hair on fire.

Miranda had seen it first, true. And, more importantly, Miranda was the one with the credit card. She was also the one with the identity crisis, Harper reminded herself. Harper was just along for the ride—she was supposed to sit by and watch, do the loyal and supportive friend thing. But Harper wasn't very good at being the sidekick—it was one of the reasons she and Miranda worked so well together. Their friendship only had room for one star, and usually Miranda was more than willing to let Harper bask in the spotlight while she waited in the wings.

"It's . . . it's not really you, Rand," Harper pointed out. And that much was true, at least. Miranda's fashion choices usually ran to white V-necked T-shirts and jeans, with the occasional brightly colored tank thrown in on days she was feeling a little wild.

"That's the idea," Miranda pointed out, her smile widening. She turned slowly in front of the mirror, craning her neck to try to get a glimpse of what she looked like from behind.

It was a contortion that Harper knew well, and she

knew exactly what Miranda was looking for—or, rather, looking at.

"Is that the right size?" Harper asked innocently. "It looks a little tight across your . . . hips."

"You think?" Miranda asked, twisting herself around even farther. "It feels okay, but—oh God, it's my ass, isn't it? You can say it. All this brown just makes it look huge."

Harper bit her lip. "It's not *huge*, exactly."

That was also strictly the truth, Harper told herself. Though it's possible the message could have been delivered in a more confident tone. Miranda was only a few pounds beyond stick thin, but for some reason, when she looked in the mirror, all she saw was flab and cellulite. Harper hated to encourage her, but how could she just sit there and watch an outfit like that walk out of the store in someone else's bag?

"It's just . . ." She let her voice trail off and gave Miranda an apologetic smile.

"Ugh, I knew it," Miranda cried. "Look at me—I look like a tree! She flicked the low, loose green top with her index finger. "Big, thick trunk and a slutty green top. Great."

"You do *not* look like a tree," Harper assured her, half laughing and half kicking herself for getting Miranda started down this road. "It looks good, really," she insisted.

Too little, too late.

Miranda was already back inside the dressing room, and soon Harper saw the shirt and skirt drop to the floor. She looked at them longingly. She could always save up some money, come back in a few weeks—if they were still there. . . .

"I don't know what I was thinking," Miranda's disembodied voice complained from behind the curtain. "Sorry I wasted your time with this stupid trip."

She came out, in her own clothes, and extended a hand to Harper, hoisting her up off the ground. "Let's just get out of here."

"You're not getting *anything*?" Harper asked in disbelief. There went three hours of her life she'd never get back—and with nothing to show for it.

"Just this," Miranda sighed, holding up a shirt that was almost identical to the one she was wearing.

So—nothing to show for it except a pain in her ass from sitting on the floor and a white V-necked T-shirt that she didn't even get to take home with her. Not that she would have wanted it.

Miranda slung an arm around Harper's shoulder.

"Screw the shopping," she said, leading her friend out of the fitting area. "Let's go get some coffee. My treat."

Harper took one last longing glance at the pile of clothes dumped in the corner of her best friend's dressing room. Too bad she and Miranda couldn't be combined into a single person—with her body and Miranda's wallet, they'd be looking pretty damn good.

Harper slipped a hand into the pocket of her fake Diesel jeans, just in case a few crisp twenty-dollar bills had decided to magically appear.

Nope.

"Coffee it is," she agreed. "Definitely your treat."

Grace wasn't a Starbucks kind of town. Big shock. If you wanted coffee, you had two choices. You could drink the black sludge they dished out at the diner, or you could step inside an unassuming and unnamed hole in the wall in the center of town and drink the finest blends this side of the Mississippi. The neon sign out front said only HOT COFFEE. (Or rather, it read HO CO FE .) But if you were a local—and in Grace, who wasn't a local?—you knew it as Bourquin's, after its owner, an angry, rotund woman who went by Auntie Bourquin. No one knew her first name—and no one had the nerve to ask. Auntie Bourquin was slow and surly, and her establishment was cramped and not too clean—but the coffee was delicious, and the fresh baked goods that appeared every morning tasted like chocolate heaven.

Miranda, who was feeling worn, deflated, and ugly after her unsuccessful bout with the shopping gods, had every reason to hope that a steaming diet mochaccino and an oversize chocolate chip cookie (it was the constant and bitter irony of her life that feeling fat and ugly made her want to run for the cookie jar) would cheer her up. They didn't call it comfort food for nothing.

But comfort wasn't in the cards.

"Do you see what I see?" Miranda hissed to Harper as soon as they'd stepped inside the coffee shop. At Harper's clueless look, Miranda jerked her head toward the far wall, where Beth was huddled over a stack of notebooks, clearly studying her bland little heart out. Not a big surprise. The surprise was sitting across from her—and his name was Kane. She pulled Harper back out the door, hoping they hadn't been seen. "What's *he* doing with *her*?"

"Calm down, she's just tutoring him for the SATs," Harper said impatiently. "Can we please go back inside now?"

"*She's* tutoring him?" Miranda asked incredulously.

"What's the difference?"

Harper could be so dense sometimes. Miranda knew that when Kane looked at her, he didn't see some babe he was desperate to bed. She knew he probably didn't even see someone he was that eager to be friends with (fortunately for her, he was stuck with her by default—she and Harper were pretty much a package deal). But she'd always thought that he'd at least seen her as a brain. Who did he call when he needed to copy some homework? Who did he go to when he needed to cheat on a test?

Miranda, that's who. It had been her one thing, and she had always hoped that someday it might be her in. It was, if nothing else, a start.

So what had changed?

"The difference is, if he needed someone to tutor him, why didn't he just ask me?" Miranda asked, staring at the two of them through the window. They were laughing about something, and she saw Kane briefly touch Beth's arm. And she knew. "He's after her, isn't he?"

"Don't be ridiculous," Harper said quickly. "She's dating one of his best friends. Even Kane wouldn't stoop that low."

"But look at them in there," Miranda said dubiously.

"Miranda, if he were after her, I would know. I promise."

"I still don't understand what he's doing with her," she complained. "They're not even friends." And she wanted very much for it to stay that way. As far as she was concerned, she had one—and only one—advantage over the bimbos Kane constantly draped himself with. They were bimbos—and Miranda wasn't. So if he ever got tired of making conversation with beautiful airheads, if he ever wanted a real relationship with a real girl, where else would he look but his old friend Miranda? Or, at least, that was her secret hope. But it all depended on the fact that, aside from Harper, Miranda was the only girl of substance he really knew—until now. For all Beth's blandness, she was sharp, serious. Real. If he befriended tall, slim, beautiful Beth, if she was in his life when he finally stopped playing the field—then Miranda's last, best hope was dead.

"I'm sure it's nothing, Rand, really," Harper assured her. "Can we go in now?"

But Miranda shook her head and turned away without a word, walking back over to the car. Her appetite was gone.

They had spent two hours buried in books, digging their way through algebra equations and an endless list of synonyms for good and evil. And there was still so much more to do. Beth felt the familiar flutter of panic as she began to think about the massive number of practice questions she needed to get through and strategies she needed to memorize before the big test—but somehow, everything seemed a little less daunting than before. Maybe because, thanks to Kane, she was no longer alone. Maybe because he'd bought her a mug of chocolate milk and a fresh-baked chocolate chip cookie, the best in town. (It was a little juvenile, Beth knew, but her sweet tooth demanded daily chocolate intake, and nothing was better than a Bourquin's cookie dipped into a frosty glass of chocolate milk. Kane had been only too happy to oblige.) Maybe it was just

Kane, sitting across the table from her, working, question-
ing, laughing—making the time fly by. They'd only had
one afternoon together, but she could already tell that
working with Kane was going to be nothing like she'd
expected.

He was nothing like she'd expected, Beth mused,
watching him up at the counter grabbing them both refills.

The Kane she knew was smug and self-absorbed, caustic and catty, and above all, lazy.

Not this Kane.

Not the guy who'd pulled out her chair for her when
she'd sat down, who'd thanked her so profusely for spending the time to tutor him, and who'd been working dili-
gently, without a break—or a single snide remark—for
more than two hours.

No, this was a complete stranger to her. But she hoped
he wouldn't be for long.

Adam flipped through the channels idly, too bored to
watch anything for more than a few seconds. It was pretty
slim pickings: a Food Channel documentary on the secrets
of cereal (hot stuff), a stupid political show . . . even ESPN
was showing some kind of greatest hits montage of old golf
shots, and who wanted to watch that? No one under the
age of sixty-five. Adam would be willing to bet on it. And
thanks to *Secrets of Las Vegas*, showing around the clock on
the Travel Channel, he now knew exactly how and where
to do so.

Just because Beth had stood him up was no reason to
spend the day lying around on the couch, counting the
cracks in the ceiling, he reminded himself. It's not like he

didn't have plenty of other friends and plenty of other options. It was just that there didn't seem to be much of a point. Why go to all that effort just to do something he didn't particularly want to do? He *wanted* to spend some time with his girlfriend. Was there something wrong with that?

So he'd told the guys to leave him out of whatever half-assed activity they'd come up with for the afternoon (last he'd checked, it had been a tie between bowling and shooting rats down at the town dump—neither a big draw, as far as he was concerned). But half-assed activity or not, he was beginning to regret the decision. Even hunting rats might be better than lying on the couch nibbling stale pizza all day.

Lucky for him—and for the rats—the phone rang.

"I thought you might be a little bored," Harper said by way of a greeting.

She didn't know the half of it.

"I just ran into Kane and Beth at the coffee shop," she continued, "and figured you might need someone to play with."

Adam's stomach clenched, but he forced himself to ignore it. He also forced himself—and it took a significant mental and physical effort—not to request any details. So what if his girlfriend and his best friend were getting cozy over coffee while he played couch potato?

"She's tutoring him for the SATs," Adam explained gruffly.

"I heard that," Harper said in a perky voice. "It's so nice of her—I know how *busy* she always is. It's great that she made the time for him."

Drive the knife in a little deeper, why don't you, he thought, but struggled to keep his irritation in check. After all it's not like any of this was Harper's fault.

"You know Beth," he offered half-heartedly.

"She just can't say no," Harper agreed.

Interesting choice of words, Adam mused. Lately, it seemed that "no" was the only word in Beth's vocabulary. At least when it came to him. When it came to the questions that counted.

But that, too, wasn't Harper's fault.

"So I'm bored," he admitted. "What are you going to do about it?"

"Funny you should ask. . . ."

Freshly showered and changed from his ratty Lakers shirt and boxers into jeans and a slightly less ratty Red Sox shirt, Adam met Harper in his driveway, and they drove to the 8 Ball, a pool hall on the outskirts of town. The place was reliably empty on a Sunday afternoon, except for a few die-hard pool sharks and a deathly pale, spiky haired bartender with a thick snake tattoo coiled around the length of his right arm. He waved at Harper as she came in, and Harper grinned back, giving him a sly wink.

"You *know* that guy?" Adam asked. But she'd already left his side, flitting over to the bar to order them a pitcher of beer. With a bemused shrug, he followed behind and slid into a seat at the bar next to her as she poured them both a mug of Pabst. It was crap, but it was also five dollars a pitcher—three on Sunday afternoons. The large wooden sign on the wall read CONSERVE WATER: DRINK BEER—and Adam was only too happy to oblige.

"So, you come here often?" he asked Harper, leering as if it were a pickup line.

"I get around," Harper, reminded him. Like everyone else she knew, Harper had a fake ID—not that you needed one in a place like Grace. It was one of those towns where everyone knew everyone else—which meant every bartender in town knew Harper and her friends were underage. Fortunately, it was also one of those towns where none of them cared.

"I just had no idea this was your kind of place," he admitted, raising his glass to her (once he'd managed to peel it off the mysteriously sticky tabletop).

"There's a lot you don't know about me," she pointed out, laughing. She downed her beer, then leaped up and tugged him toward one of the pool tables. "Come on, hotshot, time to show me your moves."

"I don't know . . . ," Adam hedged. Harper in competitive high gear wasn't a pleasant sight to see. (After losing a close game of Monopoly in third grade, she'd accused him of cheating, then stuffed two game pieces—the metal thimble and top hat—up his nose.)

"I'll go easy on you," she promised. "What—are you afraid of losing to a girl? Chicken?" She started clucking and flapping her arms, and soon the couple next to them— Adam assumed it was a couple, though he couldn't tell the man from the woman—turned to stare.

"Enough, woman!" he roared in mock anger, throwing his arms around her from behind in a tight bear hug. "You asked for it." He lifted her off the ground easily and carried her over to one of the pool tables. She squealed and kicked her feet in the air, but it was no use.

"I'll only let go if you promise to behave," he warned her, depositing her in front of one of the tables.

"As if I'd ever promise to do that," she giggled, and despite the fact that her arms were pinned to her sides, she began to tickle him—after years of practice, she knew exactly the right spots. Adam shivered with laughter and let go immediately, backing away. She smacked him affectionately on the butt and grabbed a pool cue.

"Enough playing around, mister. Let's get down to business."

Harper leaned over the pool table, drew the cue back, and, in a single, graceful sweep, knocked it into the cue ball, hitting it dead center. She paused, her chest grazing the soft green felt, her ass only a few inches away from Adam, who hovered behind her waiting for the shot and, she hoped, admiring the way she filled out her dark, snug jeans. The cue ball slammed into the eight ball and sent it skidding across the table into the far corner pocket, exactly as she'd planned.

Victory!

She spun to face Adam, who shook his head in rueful defeat.

"I give up, Harper," he said, throwing his arms up in surrender. "Three games in a row? You're clearly a better man than I."

"Let's not forget the two darts games in the middle," Harper pointed out. One of the things she loved about Adam was that he knew how to lose (of course, another thing she loved was that it was a skill he didn't need to use very often). "What can I say? I came, I saw, I conquered."

And this was different from the rest of her life how? "You came close in that last game," she conceded, softening a bit.

"Yeah, real close," Adam said sarcastically, rolling one of his striped balls into a corner pocket. There were still four left on the table.

"What? Can I help it that I'm a natural?" Harper asked with a grin.

"Yeah, yeah, come on, champ—let me buy you a victory drink before I take you home."

He grabbed her hand and led her to the bar, and Harper took a deep breath, glad he was a step ahead and couldn't see the way her face lit up at the touch of his fingers on hers. They'd had such a long, amazing afternoon, laughing and bickering and horsing around. Not flirting— for how could you flirt with someone you'd known your whole life? Flirting required some air of mystery, the sense that you were hiding more than you were revealing, the possibility that a look, a word, a touch all meant more than you were willing to admit. With Adam, everything was transparent, every move anticipated and understood.

Not that she didn't have her secrets, of course. There was the small fact that she was hopelessly in love with him. The smaller fact that she was conspiring to send his girlfriend into the arms of another guy.

But when they were together, and things were going well, stuff like that disappeared. It was like she could stop hiding, stop strategizing, stop anticipating, and just *be*. Not "be herself," because who was the "real" Harper Grace after all? Who knew? Who cared? No, with Adam, she didn't have to worry about being herself—but she didn't have to be someone else, either, like she did for the losers at school. Being popular was like a 24/7 game of Let's Pretend. It didn't matter to them who she really was—all that mattered was who she needed to be. Who she *appeared* to be.

With Adam, it was different. *She* was different. She was, they were, Harper-and-Adam, a seamless organism different and somehow better than either one alone. And there were times, when she caught a look in his eye or felt the comfortable weight of his arm around her waist, that she knew he felt it too. She could read him like that. Completely.

They were, thus, way beyond flirting.

Unfortunately, the same could not be said for Chip, the scrawny bartender-cum-bouncer-cum-heavy-metal-wannabe-boy-toy grinning at her from behind the scratched-up bar. Chip was cute enough, and useful—one of the reasons she'd gotten so good at pool was that Chip could always be counted on for a few free drinks, making the 8 Ball a perfect late-night pit stop. Once, in a fit of alcoholic gratitude, she'd even agreed to a date. Big mistake. Now he couldn't stop leering at her, and unless she wanted to start paying for her beer, she couldn't afford not to flirt back. Besides, how painful could unadulterated adoration be? And if Adam happened to notice how easily she could turn a guy on? Well, so much the better.

When they reached the bar, Chip ignored Adam, who was attempting to order. Beer for Harper, soda for him—he was too conscientious to drive drunk. Such an adorably good boy. Chip eventually nodded absentmindedly in response to Adam's request, and filled a glass with beer, never taking his eyes off Harper.

"How you doin', beautiful?" he asked, grazing his fingers along hers as he handed her the glass. His eyes dipped down from her face to her cleavage, blatantly enough that even Adam noticed—she could tell by the way he stiffened next to her. She loved it. He was priming himself to defend her honor. Perfect.

"Better, now," Harper replied, taking a demure sip and smiling up at Chip through lowered eyes.

"You're looking better than ever, I'll tell you that much."

Harper flicked her hair away from her face and giggled. "I bet you say that to all the girls."

"Can I get that soda now?" Adam cut in.

Chip studiously ignored him. "So, when you gonna let me take you out again, gorgeous?"

"Sooner than you think," Harper said playfully, noting the horrified look Adam shot her. "When Prada goes on sale at Wal-Mart" would have been a more accurate response—Harper shuddered, remembering the hot blast of Chip's garlicky breath on her neck—but that was no reason to spoil all the fun.

"Seriously, my soda?" Adam growled.

"Dude, tell your *friend* here to chill out," Chip complained. "What are you doing with him, anyway? Sweet piece of ass like you shouldn't be wasting your time with Joe Quarterback."

Adam jumped off his stool and took a menacing step toward the bar, where he loomed over the twerpy Chip, who, even in his pseudo-hip platform sneakers still looked about as tall as his name implied. "What did you call her?" Adam asked dangerously.

Chip seemed too stoned—or too stupid—to notice the tone. Harper smiled and sat back, ready to watch the show.

"What, you telling me you don't want to hit that?" Chip asked, gesturing toward Harper. "I know I did—and let me tell you, once isn't enough."

Adam opened his mouth and shut it again, whirling on Harper.

"Are you telling me that you and, and this—" He turned back to Chip, groping for the right words. Harper could have supplied a few choice ones, all accurate—pipsqueak, mouthbreather, pencil dick—but this was Adam's show.

"Look, asshole, say something like that about her again, and I'll—"

"Like what?" Chip sneered up at him. "Like what a luscious body she has? How good she looks in those jeans? Or how good she looks *out* of them?"

"That's it. We're getting out of here." Adam pulled Harper off the stool with one hand and grabbed his wallet with the other. He tore out a five-dollar bill and threw it down on the bar.

Chip slid it back toward him roughly.

"Oh no, my treat."

"Take it," Adam growled, pushing it back toward him.

"I *said*, it's on me."

"You know what? Have it your way." Adam grabbed the bill back and lifted Harper's half-full glass of beer in a mock toast. "It's on you." And he dumped the beer on Chip's head, grabbing Harper and pulling her out of the bar before the dim-witted loser's reflexes had time to kick him into motion.

"What the hell did you just do in there, Ad?" Harper asked, gasping with laughter, once they were safely out in the parking lot. "I can never show my face in there again!"

"He was asking for it," Adam said, stone-faced. "And you!" He shook his head. "I know you've dated some losers in your time, but this guy?"

"Well, Chip's an idiot," Harper admitted, "but he's got a few other things going for him."

"Stop." Adam lightly covered her mouth with his hand. "Please, I don't want to hear it."

She batted her eyelashes up at him. "What? Jealous?"

"Oh, please," he scoffed. "Just get in the car."

She laughed, and did as he said. She didn't have to press the point—because she knew she was right.

He'd fought for her honor.

He'd been jealous, jealous of the idea of her with another guy.

Which meant that somewhere in that thick and oblivious head of his was buried the knowledge that she really belonged to him. That somewhere beneath all those layers of puppy dog love for Beth and all that "just friends" bullshit he reserved for Harper, he wanted something more.

He wanted her.

She knew it.

He just needed a little push in the right direction. And he was about to get it.

chapter

4

Kaia skipped lunch on Monday. It was no big loss. After a month in this hick-filled hellhole, she'd learned that the less Grace-produced food ingested, the better. Besides, Kaia had other things on her mind. One in particular.

He wasn't in his classroom, but she found him a few minutes later in the so-called "faculty lounge," really a dark, oversize closet with a few threadbare couches and a malfunctioning coffee machine.

Students weren't allowed in the room—it was to be a sanctuary for the underpaid burnouts whose snoozing students failed to see the applicability of algebra to a future career in tractor-pulling, or the ability of Shakespeare to improve their application to the beauty academy. Two years ago the teachers had gone on strike, demanding shorter hours, fewer students per class, more pay; they'd received a faculty lounge.

Kaia didn't know any of that, of course, but if she had, she wouldn't have cared.

She did know she wasn't supposed to go inside. The boldfaced NO STUDENTS sign on the door was a good tip-off. The sharp glare Mrs. Martin shot her as she scuttled out of the lounge was a better one. Teachers-only territory. No trespassing.

Kaia didn't care about that, either. She pushed through the door into the dark space, and there he was, Jack Powell—adorable, and alone.

At first he didn't see her. He was sprawled on one of the couches, reading by the dim light of a halogen lamp—the overhead lighting was about as much use as a half-dead flashlight when it came to lighting up the room, much less the page. He'd kicked his legs up on the makeshift coffee table and was poring over a thick hardcover, his face scrunched up in thought. He was completely absorbed, and failed to notice when the door swung open. It was left to Kaia to break his concentration.

"Greetings and salutations, Mr. Powell," she said in a low voice.

He looked up with an expression of absentminded bemusement; it disappeared as soon as he paired the voice with her face. He snapped the book shut in anger and quickly stood, backing away from her.

"Did I not make myself clear the last time we spoke, Ms. Sellers? Get out of here."

"Don't trust yourself alone with me?" she taunted him. "Worried about what you might do?"

"I'm not the one who's worried—thanks to you, I've got half the school thinking I want to play Humbert Humbert to your Lolita. But I'm sure you know that already, since it's exactly what you wanted."

"All I ever wanted was you, Mr. Powell," she said sweetly. "Didn't *I* make myself clear?"

"Crystal. Now, did anyone see you come in here?"

"Only Mrs. Martin," she admitted.

"Well, that's just great." He shook his head and raised his eyes to the ceiling in exasperation. "She'll have half the town ready to lynch me if she figures out we were in here together. You have to get out of here. Now."

"You're sounding a little desperate there, Mr. Powell— it's not very becoming." That was a lie, actually. The sharp edge of desperation in his voice made the whole hard-to-get act even sexier.

He paused and gave her a piercing look. It was the same intent gaze he'd given her in their very first encounter, just before explaining that even if she hadn't been "trouble dressed up in a miniskirt," he made it a policy not to get involved with students. That had been before she caught him trying to get "involved" with Beth, of course—it turned out the only students he stayed away from were the ones he saw as potential threats. She was too hot to handle, apparently—which was infuriating. And flattering.

"Kaia, you seem like a bright girl," he finally said. "Bright enough to know that you can make life here rather uncomfortable for me."

"I'm glad you noticed."

"So I'll assume you're bright enough to understand that *I* can make life rather uncomfortable for *you*," he pointed out. "I could, for one, fail you."

"I could say it was sexual harassment," she countered. "Retribution."

"I could say it was your word against mine."

"I could say that's attacking the victim."

"And I could say the same—so it would seem we're at an impasse."

"Why, Mr. Powell," she asked flirtatiously, "are you suggesting a truce?"

He slumped back down on the couch and began massaging his temples. "Kaia, I'm not the one who declared a war," he reminded her. "I'm suggesting you drop this whole thing, drop my class if you can, do whatever it takes for you to walk out this door and out of my life forever."

"You'd miss me," she chirped.

"I doubt it."

"What would you do for fun without me?"

"I suspect I'd find something else," he said wearily. "Something that didn't cause blinding headaches and nausea."

Any more of this sweet talk and she was going to get a cavity.

"Okay, I'll go," she allowed. "For now. But I should point out that when you say we're at an impasse, you're forgetting two things."

"Enlighten me."

"One." She ticked it off on one of her fingers. "You're right that it would be your word against mine, and maybe my word's not worth too much around here. But *Beth's* is. And something tells me she might have some interesting things to say on the subject."

He stood up again—but suddenly seemed slightly unsteady on his feet. "Is this your ham-handed way of threatening to blackmail me, Kaia?" It sounded tough, but she knew she'd shaken him. Good. Now they both under-stood that she had the upper hand.

"No—let's call it a demonstration of goodwill," she offered. "Because for the moment, I'm planning to keep my mouth shut. You're the only person who knows what I saw. And for the moment, I'm willing to keep it that way."

"And why, pray tell, is that?"

For one thing, she'd decided that this was the kind of information that could keep. Why use it now when she could get what she needed out of him first? She'd save this for when it counted. But an honest answer wouldn't do much to help her cause.

"Well, that would be point number two," she told him, ticking off a second finger. "I like you, Jack Powell. I think you've got a lot of . . . possibilities. So I'm going to keep quiet about Beth. I'm going to walk out of here and show you that I can be as discreet as any of the adoring goody-goody students I'm sure you've wooed into bed in the past—but I'm not giving up. I have a lot of patience when it comes to getting what I want."

"And what about what I want?" he asked drily.

"You don't need patience," she pointed out. "I'm right here. You just need to come and get me."

They'd needed somewhere out of the way, somewhere no one they knew would ever be or would ever think to look for them. The school library was an obvious choice. Huddled over a small table in the back (sandwiched in the stacks between self-help and pet grooming), Harper and Kane quickly got down to business.

"It's a good start, Grace, but we need to kick it into

higher gear. Slow and steady's not going to win us the race on this one," Kane whispered.

Harper craned her neck around, once again making sure that no one she knew could overhear them. Her crowd wasn't much for the musty book zone, it was true—but a certain brainy Barbie clone had been known to stop by.

"I don't know, Kane—that relationship has a definite expiration date. And with Beth fawning all over you for the next two weeks, maybe . . ."

"Adam will have enough space to discover you're the best thing ever to happen to him?" Kane finished for her.

Harper blushed. That was, in fact, exactly what she'd been thinking. "Well, if you want to put it that way."

"Wake up, Harper," Kane said sharply, snapping his fingers in front of her face. "These two could go on like this indefinitely. They're both too noble to cut their losses. I know Adam, and he's going to stay in this to the bitter end, and Beth—"

"Couldn't stand on her own two feet if you nailed them to the floor and shoved a pole up her—"

"Hey, watch how you talk about my woman."

"*Your* woman?" She arched an impeccably plucked eyebrow. "Someone's getting a little ahead of himself."

"Exactly my point—I don't like waiting, and I didn't think you did either. Isn't that why we're in this thing?"

"Okay," she conceded. "So we've got the setup, Adam's already jealous—"

"And soon it will start to fester—," Kane added.

"Especially if we help it along a bit," Harper concluded. *So* not a problem. If there was one thing she could handle, it was feeding the flames of jealousy—hadn't she proved that well enough over the weekend? "But we need something else, something more dramatic, with a little flair."

"I couldn't agree more. But what?" Kane asked. They were right back to where they'd started. "That's the million-dollar question. And it has to be done right, with finesse— we don't want this to backfire."

"Are you thinking of something specific?"

"I'm just trying to ensure that we *both* get what we want," Kane explained, winking, "since, never let it be said I think only of myself . . ."

Harper raised both eyebrows this time.

"Okay, usually I do," he admitted. "But in this case, we're in it together—one for all, all for one, et cetera."

"Whatever, I'll believe it when I see it. I've known you for too long."

"Oh, you wound me!" he exclaimed. Mrs. Martin, the ancient and evil-eyed librarian, walked by and gave them a nasty look. The shut-up-or-get-out kind of look. Harper lowered her eyes and tried to muster a chaste and innocent smile. But Mrs. Martin, immune to the act, just scuttled on by.

"I'm supposed to trust you?" Harper asked, lowering her voice to a whisper. "When you're trying to steal your best friend's girlfriend?"

All traces of a smirk vanished from Kane's face, and he glared at her with hooded eyes.

"First of all, Grace, I don't believe in trust—which is why I don't believe in best friends. It's easier that way. And second of all, as for stealing his girlfriend . . ."

Harper leaned forward eagerly. She'd been wondering how Kane could justify his scheming, especially when he seemed to have no particular motivation for choosing Beth, of all the girls he could have pursued.

". . . let's just say—karma's a bitch."

"Care to elaborate?" Harper asked.

"No."

They stared at each other in silence for a moment, each daring the other to speak. Harper broke first.

"Fine—just get back to what you were saying," Harper urged him. "What kind of backfiring are you afraid of?"

"Well, we could pin something on Adam, like, say, he slept with someone else—believable enough, I guess," Kane said, his smirk returning. "Deep down, all guys are pigs."

Harper opened her mouth—then closed it again. She couldn't betray Adam's confidence. At least not until she heard all of what Kane had to say.

"That could work," she mused.

He shook his head slowly but surely. "Not so much—think about it. Beth breaks up with Adam in a fit of anger, and Adam spends the rest of his life trying to win her back. And I don't think either of us wants to deal with that."

"Agreed," Harper said, her heart sinking. He was right—and she had nothing. Nothing that wouldn't turn Harper and Adam's potential relationship into collateral damage. "In fact, I think Adam needs to be the one to break it off," she concluded in spite of herself. "He feels betrayed, she feels unjustly wronged, they both want nothing to do with each other and go running into our arms."

"Sounds like the perfect plan. Except . . ." Kane sighed

in exasperation. "We still need to figure out how to get from point A to point B."

"We'll figure it out," she comforted him. "In the meantime we continue to drive Adam out of his mind with jealousy?"

"You got it. And, hey, never underestimate the power of the Kane Geary charisma. For all I know, a couple more of these study 'dates' and she'll be begging *me* to hit the bedroom."

Harper balled up a piece of paper and tossed it at his big, fat head. "Leaving Adam ready and waiting for some sympathetic TLC from his beautiful next door neighbor?" she suggested sarcastically. "Unlikely."

"Hey, you never know—it could happen."

It's not like Miranda had no one to eat lunch with. No, she reassured herself, she had plenty of friends. Just because Harper had randomly decided to skip out on lunch didn't mean Miranda was adrift on some sea of loserdom. There were plenty of people she *could* sit with, plenty who would covet her presence at their table if only because the reflected beams of Harper's glory made Miranda glow with the light of borrowed popularity. But the prospect of pushing "food" around on her tray while listening to the stupid simpering of these so-called friends—without Harper across the table to exchange timely eye rolls with—was just too much for her to handle this afternoon. So instead, Miranda opted for a snack machine lunch (granola bar and mini canister of Pringles) at the newspaper office, which had a door that locked and a couch that creaked noisily but had yet to collapse.

But first, a pit stop at the girls' bathroom. She stood in front of the mirror, touching up her makeup—and making a mental note that a makeup makeover would definitely have to be the next stop on her road to self-improvement. The peach frosted lip gloss and smoky gray eye shadow she'd picked out in tenth grade just wouldn't do. Her mother, though usually having more than enough to say on the subject of Miranda's appearance—and how to improve it—knew nothing about makeup herself. She'd been able to contribute very little to Miranda's education on the subject beyond such helpful pointers as "That blush makes you look like a whore."

The bathroom was surprisingly uncrowded for this time of day. A couple stoners lurked in the back corner, from the sound of it competing over who had more Phish bootlegs. A cluster of super-skinny bottle blondes—Miranda didn't recognize them, so figured they must be freshmen—hogged most of the mirror area, reapplying their hairspray and shimmery lipstick. From the short skirts to the perfect manicures to the cocky tilt of their heads Miranda could tell they were jockeying for a place in the line of succession, ready to fill the power vacuum once Harper had graduated. *Cosmo* clones, Miranda thought disdainfully. They could look the part all they wanted, but they'd never have that spark, that something special Harper had that made people want to follow her to the ends of the earth (or at least to the end of good judgment). Harper was a leader. These girls—it was obvious—were sheep.

And yet . . .

And yet, she thought, looking from one perfectly sculpted and outfitted body to the next, wasn't this exactly the look she was craving?

Long, silky smooth hair that could bounce and blow in the wind—Miranda's hair was brittle, thin, and impossibly flat. Flawless complexions—Miranda had zits and freckles. Long, slim, tanned legs—Miranda's thunder thighs were albino pale.

The girls bustled out of the bathroom, chattering about who had hooked up that weekend and who was feeling fat. Big surprise—unanimous responses to both.

Miranda sighed and considered trying to score some pot off the stoners in the corner, anything to calm the rising tide of anxiety she suddenly felt at the daunting prospect of finding a way to turn herself into *that*. Not that she wanted to be vapid, of course. But beautiful? Stylish? *Skinny?* The kind of girl who screams "high maintenance" but which, it seemed, was all any worthwhile guy wanted?

Yes, please.

Haven High was a small school. Claustrophobically small, it sometimes seemed to Adam. But he'd done a decent job so far of avoiding Kaia. He hadn't spoken to her, in fact, since their last encounter. He still shuddered at the thought of it—the intense, mind-blowing sex in an abandoned motel, followed almost immediately by an utterly humiliating blow-off. What a loser he'd been. He saw that now. It was too late, of course—he'd done it, this huge, horrible thing that weighed on him, crushed him, and yet still flickered through his fantasies, taunting him with what he couldn't have yet still, in some deep part of him, wanted.

Beth had wondered why he suddenly stopped following Kaia around and inviting her out with the group, but she had no fond feelings for Kaia herself, so hadn't wondered very long or very loudly. And maybe she didn't want to know.

Still, it was a small school, and he'd been bound to bump into Kaia eventually. He just hadn't counted on a literal collision.

"Oh, sorry!" he exclaimed, after spinning away from his locker and slamming into someone rushing past him down the hall. Then—"Oh, it's you." Suddenly, the split-second collision became, in his mind, an embrace, as if he could still feel the ghostly touch of his body pressing against hers, their hands and chests and hips awkwardly rubbing against each other, her silky hair whipping across his face.

"And it's you, too," she pointed out. "Where've you been, stranger?"

"Far away from you, which I thought was how you wanted it." Her words to him at their last meeting echoed through his head. And the mocking laughter.

"Oh, Adam, I hope I didn't hurt your feelings." She placed a soft hand on his chest—he pushed it away. "I don't know what I'd do if I thought you hated me!"

"Give it up, Kaia," he said harshly. "I'm not falling for your crap again. Find someone new to screw over."

Kaia rolled her eyes. "Oh, right," she scoffed. "You're such the wounded victim, used and abused, right? You didn't seem to mind the screwing part so much."

"Shut up," he hissed, suddenly aware of the students swarming around them. Watching. Listening? "I thought we agreed you weren't going to tell anyone about that."

"Oh, calm down. My lips are sealed. Why would I do anything to get between you and your precious Beth?"

"I appreciate that, Kaia." He tried to ignore the disdainful edge to her voice. Kaia, he'd decided, was like a venomous snake—you just had to be very careful, stay very still, and wait her out until she got bored and went away.

"Of course," she added, smirking, "maybe I'm not the one you need to worry about."

"What's that supposed to mean?" he asked, against his better judgment.

"I saw your blushing rose getting cozy in the coffee shop with your supposed best friend the other day. Just thought you'd want to know."

"Old news," he said, affecting nonchalance. Ignoring the taste of bile. "She's tutoring him for the SATs. I know all about it. And it's completely innocent." And this he believed wholeheartedly, he told himself. He had to, right?

"So I heard. Such a sweet girl, to commit her time to helping him, when she's oh so busy. But totally innocent, of course," she assured him, voice dripping with false sincerity. "I'm sure you're right. Just another platonic extracurricular, like any other: yearbook, newspaper, party planning . . ."

She narrowed her gaze suggestively and Adam felt the tips of his ears turn red. It was, after all, planning a party that had brought Adam and Kaia together in the first place. A few weeks' worth of purely platonic meetings culminating in one night of illicit but extraordinary passion.

"I'm sure you have nothing to worry about, though," she said after a moment of silence. "I mean, you're in love, right? And that's what love is all about—trust."

Trust. Right.

If Beth's love for him proved as trustworthy as his love for her, they were in for some serious problems.

Job well done, Kaia congratulated herself. Adam had, of course, walked away from her in disgust, but she could see the beginnings of doubt in the nervous twist of his lip and the tiny rivulets of sweat that traced a path down the muscles of his neck. She'd gotten under his skin—again.

Kaia laughed to herself. It probably wasn't very nice of her to pick on Adam again. After all, he was such an easy mark, and clearly still smarting from their last encounter. On the other hand, she considered, she'd given him a true gift—one that he'd certainly enjoyed enough at the time, no matter how much he may now claim she'd ruined his life. Didn't she deserve to have some fun too? And if it was fun at Beth Manning's expense, even better. Much as she tried, she couldn't forget the fact that Mr. Powell had chosen that simpering softie over her. Yes, it was clearly because he thought Kaia spelled trouble, while Beth would be easy prey. Powell was a predator; it was why she liked him so much. But still, there it was—he'd rejected her in favor of Beth, and while that was a lapse in judgment she was willing to forgive, Beth still needed to pay.

This time, she'd decided, there was no reason to go it alone. Not when such a good game was already afoot.

So she headed to the library. She'd spotted Harper heading in that direction at the beginning of lunch period, and she had a sneaking suspicion she'd find her huddled over a desk with Kane, hatching some pathetic plan. It was time to lend these small-town tricksters the wisdom of her experience.

Why?

Why the hell not?

She found them just as she'd imagined, heads together, arms waving animatedly, whispers flying. She crept up slowly behind Harper, finger to her lips, trusting Kane to keep his poker face, which he did, right up to the moment that Kaia tapped Harper on the shoulder and smiled angelically into her face, which reflected, in quick succession, surprise, guilt, and disgust. Harper settled on the latter, but Kaia kept up her icy smile.

"What do you want?" Harper hissed. "We're busy here."

"I don't mind if the lovely Kaia joins us," Kane said generously.

"Shut up, Kane." Harper glared at him, then turned back to Kaia. "Why are you still here?"

"What, is this where you tell me, 'This is an *A, B* conversation, and I should *C* my way out of it?'" Kaia sneered.

"I was leaning more toward, 'This is an *X, Z* conversation, so *Y* don't you just go away," Harper corrected her. "Or at least I *would* have been if this were 1998 and we were ten years old. What do you think this is, VH1's *Lamest Slang of the '90s?*"

"Well, your outfit does say 'retro gone wrong,'" Kaia pointed out, "but I guess you're not out of time, just out of taste. I can live with that."

"I'm supposed to take fashion tips from someone who makes Paris Hilton look classy?" Harper scoffed.

Kane, whose eyes had been bouncing back and forth between the two as if he were following a heated Ping-Pong match, began to softly applaud. "Bring it on, ladies. When do we take out the mud wrestling pit?"

"Shut up, Kane," they snapped in unison.

He chuckled softly. "Okay, okay, I know when I'm not wanted." He checked his watch and stood up, collecting his books. "Besides," he gave Harper a meaningful look, "I've got to go meet someone. We're setting up a study 'date' for later. See ya."

Harper shot him a vicious, how-dare-you-leave-me-here-alone-with-*her* look, but he just grinned and disappeared.

"Such a studious guy all of a sudden," Kaia commented.

"Yeah, well, you know Kane, needs to win at all costs," Harper said uncomfortably. "Even if it means some hard work."

"It's going to be pretty damn hard to win at the rate you two are going," Kaia pointed out.

"What's that supposed to mean?"

Kaia laughed to herself. It would have been cute if it weren't so pathetic, this little show of ignorance and innocence. Harper was going to have to work on the poker face a bit if this whole thing was going to work.

"I think you know," Kaia said simply.

Harper sighed. "Kaia, it's a little early in the week for mind games, don't you think?"

"Look I didn't come here to fight, or play games," Kaia promised her, wishing they could just cut through the bullshit and skip to the part where they got something done. But, as she well knew, that's not how these things worked. And the bullshit was, in the end, half the fun. "At least, not with you."

"Then what?" Harper asked wearily.

"I know what you're up to," Kaia said, relishing the involuntary shudder that ran through Harper's body. "And I want to help."

"You know what we're up to? Are you talking in code now? What is this, a James Bond movie? What would we be 'up to'?"

"Do you really want me to spell it out for you? Adam, Beth, Operation Screw Over Your Supposed Best Friend—or, in your case, just screw him?"

Harper's face turned pale. "I don't know what you're talking about," she claimed in a strangled voice.

"Yeah, yeah, whatever you say. You're totally innocent, you're appalled I would even suggest it. Whatever." Kaia checked her watch. This was getting old. "Here's my point. I want to help—you two are playing out of your league, and I think you need some coaching from a pro. That's me."

"Just out of curiosity," and it was clear that Harper had plenty, "let's say Kane and I did have some unholy alliance—why would *you* want to help? And why would we trust you?"

"I'm helping because I'm bored, and because I hate to see a good opportunity go to waste. As for why you should trust me?" Kaia paused. It was a good question. One that deserved a reasonably honest answer. "You shouldn't. But you're going to anyway because you've got almost everything you need—will, motive, lack of scruples—but you're missing one key thing, and that's what I can supply."

"And what's that?" Harper asked skeptically.

"A plan."

chapter

5

It was Harper's policy never to have to depend on someone. Especially not because she was desperate.

She was Harper Grace.

She didn't do desperate.

At least, not usually. Under normal circumstances she plowed through the world and everyone else got out of the way. Unless you were slow. Then you just got run over. She certainly didn't need anyone's help to do it. Of course, under normal circumstances she didn't usually betray one of her best friends for the purposes of seducing the other, but these circumstances were anything but normal, and with the fate of her love life hanging in the balance, speed was of the essence. Which meant that Harper, lacking scruples and strategy in equal amount, was desperate.

And desperate times called for desperate measures . . . right?

So when Kaia stood up from the cramped library table

with an ultimatum: "Meet me after school and listen to what I have to say, or forget the whole thing," Harper had nodded. Finally, and fatefully, she had decided to give Kaia a chance.

But she wasn't about to do it anywhere near the school, where someone could see them together. Kaia's Eurotrash wardrobe, frozen beauty, and outlandish public liplock with Haven High's most eligible bachelor had won her a fair amount of notoriety, but it wasn't the kind that translated into social acceptance. She had a few followers, of course, but she was too high and mighty to inspire much loyalty, and most of the initial curiosity seekers had drifted away as Harper slowly but thoroughly put out word that the new girl was not to be touched. Someone like Kaia could have easily toppled Harper's carefully constructed high school hierarchy—so Harper did what she had to do to neutralize the threat.

When Harper spoke, people listened. And if they knew what was good for them, they obeyed.

She wasn't about to waste all that hard work by meeting with Kaia in a public place and letting the world think they were suddenly bosom buddies. Harper saw her friendship as a powerful gift, and Christmas for Kaia wasn't coming anytime soon.

So she needed a place where no one—*no one*—would recognize her, where no one she knew would ever deign to set foot. Hence: the Cactus Cantina. A greasy Tex-Mex bar with Cheez Whiz nachos and double-shot margaritas, the Cactus was good for inducing a heart attack or drinking yourself into oblivion, but little else.

Harper was already seated (albeit gingerly—she had no

interest in letting any part of her body touch the mysterious sticky patches that dotted the booth) when Kaia arrived. So she got a good look at the cover girl's face when she walked in the door. It wasn't pretty. Or, rather—this being Kaia—it was spectacularly pretty. But it was prettiness scrunched up into a grimace of horror and reticence, her whole body telegraphing a single message: Dear God, don't make me go in there. Please.

She stood in the door for a moment, half in, half out, and a shaft of light sliced into the darkness, sending up a groan of discomfort from the bowels of the bar.

"Yer in or yer out, senorita," the bartender with the fake Zapata mustache called to Kaia. She flinched at the scraping sound of his voice. "Make up your mind, *por favor.*"

Harper waited and watched. It was the first test of Kaia's commitment to the cause—and, to her credit, she passed.

"Was *this* really necessary?" she asked Harper, sitting down across from her.

"What?" Harper tried her best to look comfortable, though not *too* comfortable, as if this world were foreign but unintimidating—and especially as if she weren't planning to take a shower the moment she got out of there to wash the stench out of her hair. The goal had been to throw Kaia off balance, to make sure she was out of her element—a plan which, by all appearances, had worked like a charm. Harper would just have to deal, and keep her own squirming and scowling to a minimum.

"This *place*," Kaia said, waving her arms in elaboration, as if to encompass the cardboard lizards and cacti papering the walls, the tinny salsa soundtrack, and the seedy denizens all in one sweep. "Or is this just your thing?"

Harper shrugged, affecting unconcern. "You're the one who thinks Kane and I have this dirty little plan," she pointed out. "I would think you'd understand the need to be a little discreet."

"Whatever." Kaia grabbed a napkin and gingerly flicked away the mysteriously colored crumbs littering her side of the table. "I take it we're getting right down to business?"

"I'm done with small talk if you are."

"Good." She leaned forward, and Harper was once again taken by her perfect form and poise, even in a place like this. And that rust-colored asymmetrical shirt? It was unmistakably a Betsey Johnson original. Harper closed her eyes for a moment and, with a sharp pang of envy, briefly considered what it would be like to have Kaia's life—but she couldn't even begin to imagine.

"Here's how I see it," Kaia continued. "You want Adam. Kane—for whatever reason—wants Beth. You teamed up to split them up, and you're ready and waiting for them to fall, heartbroken and sobbing, into your arms. How am I doing so far?"

Harper was disgusted with herself. Some secret plan. What a joke. And it sounded even more pathetic coming out of Kaia's mouth. But she played it off. She had to.

"So far you haven't told me anything I don't know," she complained.

"I'll take that to mean, 'Why, yes, Kaia, that's the situation exactly. Please enlighten me as to how to make my dreams come true.'"

"I'm listening."

"So you've got Beth tutoring Kane—a nice move, incidentally, but Adam's too much of a wuss to break up with her just because he's jealous. He'd never trust his own instincts on that one—and princess Beth isn't going to fall on Kane unless you push her."

"Again, waiting for the newsflash," Harper drawled, inwardly bristling at the way Kaia casually spoke of Adam's flaws and failings, as if she knew him so well.

"Well, for one thing, what you may not know is that Adam has some secrets of his own that Beth might not be too happy to hear." A secretive smile crept across Kaia's face. Harper knew exactly what she was referring to, but any pleasure she might have drawn from taking Kaia down a peg was hollow. She'd caught a glimpse of Kaia-and-Adam, act one, and had yet to wash the painful images out of her mind. She didn't like to be reminded of act two, when they'd adjourned to a bedroom; Harper had, mercifully, missed the fireworks. But she could imagine. And did—often.

"Yeah, yeah, he slept with you," Harper said, the words slicing into her. "Big deal. Anyway, I can't use it."

Kaia's eyes widened, and Harper smiled, knowing that at least she'd taken the wind out of the other girl's sails, as hoped. But Kaia wasn't thrown off for long.

"So he told you? Interesting—and not too smart."

"Well, that's Adam, honest to a fault. Of course, he used to be loyal to a fault, too," Harper said, glaring, "before *you* got through with him."

"Do you want to fight about my popping your boy's cherry, or do you want to get him for yourself?"

"What's the difference?" Harper asked irritably. "I told you, I can't use it. If Beth breaks up with him over this, he'll spend the rest of the year feeling guilty and chasing after her. That does me no good at all. And, not that I really care, but I imagine that Beth wouldn't be bouncing back too quickly either—I see her as the 'I can never trust a man again' type. After something like that, I don't think Kane would exactly be her type."

"Good thing I have a backup plan, then," Kaia said triumphantly. "One that turns Beth into the villain. Adam will be looking for a 'true' friend to turn to, and you'll be right there to pick up the pieces."

"Sounds perfect. Only one problem—Beth would never cheat on Adam. She doesn't have it in her."

"Oh, really?" Kaia smiled, and it seemed she was about to say something, but she stopped herself, paused for a moment, and then continued. "Well, I suppose you're right. And *we* know that, and *Beth* knows that, but there's no reason Adam has to. And all that really matters is what *he* believes."

"He accuses her—unjustly—she gets mad, we get mutual destruction." Harper nodded eagerly. "I like it. But how—"

She cut herself off at the sight of two drunken hulks looming over their table, one uglier than the other. (Although it was admittedly difficult to judge: Were buck teeth uglier than gold teeth? Was the jagged scar above the eyebrow uglier than an irregularly shaped red blotch covering the chin? Was mountain man hair uglier than no hair?)

Baldy leered down at the two girls, his stained T-shirt exuding the stench of cheap beer.

"You ladies are at our table," he slurred.

"'S *our* table," Mountain Man agreed. "Everyone knows that."

Baldy tried to squeeze into the booth with Harper, but with a yelp of anger and a sharp jab, she successfully pushed him away. He stumbled backward, but Mountain Man broke his fall.

"Wasn't nice," Mountain Man warned them. "You're sitting at *our* table, you must belong to us too. Move over."

Kaia wrinkled her nose and shot Harper a look of disbelief. "Why are these losers talking to us?" she asked.

Harper cringed at her choice of words—she'd spent enough time around Grace's roughnecks to know that the best tactic was to shut up and get out of the way. But she wasn't about to be bested by Kaia's bravado. So she mustered some of her own.

"I don't know—they must be as stupid as they are ugly," she said, forcing a laugh. It felt good.

"Who you calling stupid?" Baldy asked menacingly.

"You sure ain't too ugly yourself, babe," Mountain Man leered, passing his greasy hand through Harper's hair. *That* was enough. She jumped up from the table—and suddenly realized she was taller than both of them.

"Listen, buddy, get the hell out of my face," she snapped.

"Who's gonna make me? You? Or your hot little friend?"

As Harper searched for the words that would end this fiasco before it went any further, a scruffy guy about her age came wandering over.

"We got a problem here?" he asked, getting in

Mountain Man's face. "She asked you to leave her alone."

"Who asked you, shithead?" Baldy growled, stepping up behind their knight in scruffy armor.

It was over in an instant.

Scruff Boy punched Mountain Man in the gut and, before Baldy had a chance to react, gave *him* a shove hard enough to knock both men to the ground. As the two losers lumbered up to their feet and began advancing on him, they got a nasty surprise—a tap on the shoulder from the Cactus bouncer, a WWE reject who looked like he bench-pressed losers like them for a warm-up. And, apparently, a friend of Scruff Boy's.

Five minutes later the bouncer was back at the entrance, having barely broken a sweat, Mountain Man and Baldy were stumbling through the parking lot with a few fresh scars to show off to the ladies, and Scruff Boy? He was still standing there.

Harper looked him up and down—medium height, medium build, wildly curly black hair, and dark, catlike eyes. Kind of hot, really, beneath that stubble and the torn Clash T-shirt. She knew who he was, of course—she knew every guy in town. Especially the hot ones. He went to their school, barely (this was his second senior year in a row), played in a band, ran with a crowd that drank too much and smoked even more. Pretty much a total waste of space. But he had, after all, cleaned up their mess. They should probably be polite—

"Why are *you* still here?" Kaia asked him, curling her lip in disdain.

Or not.

"You two okay?" he asked, in a slow, zoned-out voice.

"I'm Reed." He stuck out his hand for Kaia to shake—she left him hanging.

"We're fine," Harper jumped in, again not to be outdone. "So you can just run off back to . . . whatever it is people like you do."

He stood frozen in place, looking at them both with a mixture of disgust and disbelief.

"What are you waiting for?" Kaia finally asked. "A medal?"

"Actually, a thank-you," he informed her. "My mistake."

"You're right. It was," Kaia said, and turned back to Harper. "What was I saying?"

Harper watched the boy out of the corner of her eye. He stood there for another moment, as if waiting for them to let him in on the joke. Then reality sank in. He shook his head and trekked back across the bar to a booth crowded with deadbeat delinquents. They pounded him on the back and slammed him with high fives—impressed by the fight, she supposed. Good thing they hadn't paid attention to the aftermath. Reed Sawyer could take on two drunken thugs with ease, but apparently in Harper and Kaia, he'd met his match.

"You were about to blow my mind with your oh-so-perfect plan," Harper prodded Kaia, putting the whole sordid incident out of her mind.

Kaia laid it out for her, step by step, and when she was done, Harper leaned back and let loose a low whistle of admiration. It was breathtakingly perfect—beautiful, and a little complex, but if everything went smoothly, it would deliver the goods. She could already imagine herself in Adam's arms.

And if Kaia really came through, and she owed all her happiness to her worst enemy? Well, if it got her Adam, it was a debt she'd be willing to spend the rest of her life repaying. And knowing Kaia, that might be exactly how long it would take.

The Wizard of Oz was playing at the Starview. It played there every year in October, and every year, Miranda and Harper went to the last showing and split a large popcorn and an overpriced box of Mike and Ikes. It was tradition, and had been ever since eighth grade, when they'd both desperately wanted to go but had been too embarrassed to admit it to each other. Finally, on the day the movie was set to close, they'd each secretly snuck off to the theater—only to run into each other in the lobby, both buying boxes of Mike and Ikes.

By now it was a ritual set in stone, down to the whispered comments they tossed back and forth during the show and the postmovie pizza and beer at Guido's. (The beer had been a tenth-grade addition, but in some cases, it was worth making a change.) It was tradition—fixed, beloved, and unbreakable. At least, until now.

Now Miranda stood at Harper's locker, waiting in vain for her friend to show, watching the minutes slip past and the other students fade from the hall, until only she stood there, patient and alone.

The movie started at five. By four, Miranda was done waiting. She'd already waited an embarrassing half hour too long.

And she wasn't about to go to the movie herself, not alone, not as if the past five years had never happened and she was still a gawky eighth grader too worried about her status to admit a geeky love for Munchkins.

No, apparently Harper had better things to do—probably some guy had sworn his everlasting love and she'd taken him out for a quick spin—"quick" being the operative word, since use 'em or lose 'em got tedious if you hesitated too long before moving from the former to the latter. Or so Harper always said.

Not that Miranda hadn't eliminated her share of lovestruck losers—it was just that the tan, dark, and handsome set didn't usually flock in her direction. At five feet one, maybe she was just too close to the ground for them to see her.

She was tired of being invisible and—apparently—forgettable. Why should Harper have all the fun? Miranda found her car, one of the last in the largely empty lot, and took off toward the strip mall on the edge of town.

Her new and improved look had waited long enough, and outfit number one was there, ready and waiting for her.

Was it too risqué? Did it make her boobs look big? Did the skirt make her ass look huge? Maybe. *So what?* she fumed silently, trying to drown out Harper's scoffing voice in her mind. At least it makes a statement. At least people will remember I'm there.

Never return to the scene of the crime. If it worked for *Law & Order*, it worked for Beth, so she'd spent the last weeks studiously avoiding the newspaper office as best she could. Every time she set foot inside, even with other people around (and she made sure there were *always* other people around), she could feel the weight of memory pressing down on her. The small space, a refurbished supply closet that she'd petitioned the school to allocate to the newspaper, had felt so cozy, so warm and familiar—a place she'd fought for and won. It had been a home. Now it was just a dank and claustrophobic cave—every time the door closed, her heart sped up, her throat constricted. She felt trapped by those walls, just like she felt in French class every time Mr. Powell's eyes alighted on her. Sometimes their gaze locked before she could look away, and she felt his eyes boring into her, the way his tongue had when his arms were wrapped around her, pushing himself against her and—

No matter what she may have been fantasizing about in her most secret, most ridiculous daydreams, she never would have acted on it. Never.

She just wished she could go back in time and make sure it never happened.

But going back not being an option, she resolved to go forward. Forward meant acing AP French, and forward meant sticking it out on the newspaper, for the sake of her college applications, if nothing else. Forward meant looking him in the eye every day and never saying anything to anyone about what had happened, until she forgot it herself. Eventually she *would* forget. It had just been a kiss. One kiss. She would forget all about it. Soon.

And today moving forward meant returning to the newspaper office, alone. Doing what she'd signed on to do—run the paper, make it great. She forced herself to return, hating the sound of her key in the door, hating the sight of the couch she used to nap on, the table at which she'd spent so many hours lost in her work. She was so different now—but everything there, it was exactly the same. And maybe in the end, she just couldn't stay away.

Neither, it seemed, could he.

She'd spent half an hour staring blankly at the computer screen, trying to finalize the page one layout for the next edition, but mainly just concentrating on keeping her body calm and still—she felt that if she relinquished control for even a moment, she'd start to tremble uncontrollably. Or just flee.

Maybe she'd known that he was on his way.

Because at the sound of the knob turning, the door opening, she didn't need to turn around—she knew it was him. Not by the jaunty footsteps or the faint whiff of his Calvin Klein cologne. She'd just known. As if the room had suddenly gotten chilly, or the walls had begun to press in.

"Beth," he said quietly.

Still she didn't turn around.

"You've been avoiding me," he said, finally.

"You noticed," she said drily, her back to him. She focused on keeping the pain and panic out of her voice—she knew, somehow, that if she could pull this off, if she could face him without crumbling, prove to both of them that she could do it, that this could be the end of it.

"Beth, if I did anything that made you feel uncomfortable . . . If you thought that I—well, sometimes it's easy for people to get the wrong idea about situations, imagine that certain things happened, when they didn't, really. Blow things out of proportion . . ."

She grabbed the edges of the desk, pressing down until the tips of her fingers faded to white, and forced herself to take a deep breath and turn around slowly.

"What is it, exactly, that you think I imagined?" she asked in a measured tone.

"Well, you obviously thought that things somehow crossed a line, and if I sent you any confusing signals, I just want to apologize—I'd just hate to see you overreact."

"Overreact?" Her voice almost broke on the last syllable, and again she forced herself to breathe. She would not yell, and she would not cry, even if it killed her. She hoped that from across the room he couldn't see that she was shaking.

"You're obviously upset," he pointed out, taking a step toward her. "If we could just—"

"Stay away," she blurted out, jumping out of her seat and away from him.

He backed off, holding his hands out in front of him as if to demonstrate they weren't hiding a secret weapon. Of course, he didn't need one.

"Okay, okay, I'm back here, okay?" he retreated to the doorway. "Just tell me, what can we do to fix things here? How can I convince you I'm not the big bad wolf?" He cocked an eyebrow and gave her a patented Jack Powell grin, and Beth suddenly realized that this was a man who'd discovered that, with his accent and his dimples, he could get away with pretty much anything.

She also suddenly realized that he needed her help to get away this time—that he was running scared. She had the power, and she could use it.

"There's nothing you can do," she said simply. "Just stay away from me. I'm not dropping out of French and I'm not dropping the newspaper—but I don't ever want to be in a room alone with you again. So make sure that doesn't happen, or I'll make sure of it for you."

He took a step toward her again.

"Are you *threatening* me?"

She was almost as surprised as he was.

"I'm just explaining things for you," she replied. "Stay away from me, or I'm going to the administration."

"And say what?" he asked, in a low, dangerous voice.

"You know what."

He came closer, and closer, until he was looming over her, only a few inches away.

"That I came on to you? That I *wanted* you? That I fell madly in love with you and you rebuffed my nefarious advances?" he hissed, curling his lip in derision. "Is that what you'll say?"

She stayed silent, lip trembling, back now pressed against the wall, eyes searching for an escape. He was blocking her path to the door.

"Because I'll tell you what I'll say," he continued. "I'll say it's a silly schoolgirl crush gone out of control. That I made the mistake of getting close to you, helping you out, not realizing what a sad, pathetic, unstable little girl you really were. Prone to tears and hallucination." He smiled coolly. "What do you think they'll say to that? Who would you believe?"

"Stop," Beth begged, hating the soft, whispery sound of her own voice. "Just stop."

"Because *I* think they'll believe me," he pressed on. "I think they'll ask themselves, why would *he* ever risk everything for someone like *her*?"

Beth had no response—it was all she could do just to stand there, stare up at him, not lose control and break down. But her control was slipping. He reached a hand toward her, and she skirted away—but there was nowhere to go.

If he touches me, I'll lose it, she realized. *I can't stop myself.*

But she couldn't stop him, either, and he smiled cruelly and put a hand on her shoulder as she felt her knees buckle and—

"Am I interrupting something in here?"

Mr. Powell jumped back from Beth and spun toward the door. Kane stood in the doorway, one arm slung against the frame, a quizzical expression painted across his face.

"That's up to Ms. Manning." Powell turned back to Beth. "Are we done here?"

"We're done," she murmured, forcing herself to meet his gaze.

"Okay, then. I'll be happy to honor your request, Ms. Manning—but I'd advise you to remember what I said here."

Beth nodded, and Mr. Powell strode out of the room. As soon as he was gone, the last of Beth's energy disappeared, and she sagged against the wall.

"What was all that about?" Kane asked, hurrying over to her. He put an arm around her and guided her to a chair. "Are you all right?"

"I'm fine," she whispered, as a tear escaped from the corner of her eye and spattered on the table.

"Okay, that's obviously a lie, but we all know I don't feel all that strongly about the truth," he said gently. "So I can deal with that."

In spite of herself, Beth smiled. "What are you doing here?" she asked, hoping he wouldn't notice her surreptitiously wiping her nose with the edge of her sleeve. She brushed another tear away.

"Looking for you, actually. Swim practice let out early, so I thought I'd come see if I could bully you into another study session. I know we weren't due to meet until tomorrow, but . . ." He grinned and pulled a brown paper bag out of his backpack. "I even brought a bribe."

She looked inside and gasped in delight.

"For me?"

"Chocolate chip cookies and chocolate milk—that's right, isn't it?"

"That's perfect."

"Somehow, I think the vending machine cookies will be slightly less satisfying than Auntie Bourquin's fresh-baked best, but I figured—"

"No, Kane, it's perfect, really. It's incredibly sweet of you to remember."

She breathed in sharply and shook herself, trying to shrug off the dark fog that had come over her. She gave him her best attempt at a smile, and pulled out a notebook, opening it up to a blank page.

"The bribe worked—let's get to it. How about we start with geometry?"

Another tear spattered onto the page, and Kane put a tentative hand on her shoulder, dropping it quickly as she instinctively jerked away.

"Beth, stop for a second."

Reluctantly, she looked up from the page, where she'd already started drawing a series of triangles.

"Are you really okay?" he asked gently. "We don't need to do this now, if you're not up for it. I can go, if you want. Or I can stay, and we can just talk."

She didn't say anything, just looked at him, wondering

how she'd missed it all these years, the sweet, sensitive look in his eyes, the soft, unquestioning openness. She'd always thought Kane was just—well, to be honest, a heartless bastard who cared only about himself. But this wasn't the face of someone who didn't care.

"Or we could just sit here and stare at each other in silence," Kane finally added. "I'm okay with that, too." He grinned. "Girls are often struck dumb by my wit and impeccable physique. It's okay, no need to be embarrassed."

She burst into laughter, and this time, she was the one to put a hand on *his* arm.

"It's okay," she told him. "We can do some work. I want to."

"Are you sure?" he asked, covering her hand with his. "Whatever it is, I just want to help."

Beth sighed, remembering the relief that had swept through her when she'd looked up to see him in the doorway, rescuing her.

"Trust me," she assured him. "You already have."

Adam froze in the doorway and just watched. Their heads bent together, his hand on hers, the grateful smile on her face.

He watched—and then he crept out as quietly as he had crept in.

Practice had let out early, and he'd thought Beth could use a pick-me-up. She'd been working so hard lately, and he knew she'd been planning to barricade herself in the newspaper office until nightfall. *Poor Beth,* he'd thought. *My poor, overworked, overstressed girlfriend.* Wouldn't it be nice to surprise her with an unexpected treat. So stupid.

He'd bought some cookies and chocolate milk from the vending machine by the gym—her favorite.

He'd rushed down the hall toward the office, already imagining the smile on her face when she saw him walk through the door, the squeal of delight at the guaranteed sugar rush. He loved to see her happy.

He'd tiptoed to the door of the office, oh-so-gently and oh-so-quietly turned the handle, eased the door open—and there they were. Kane and Beth, bent over their work together—though they obviously weren't working.

Kane was munching on a cookie, Beth was giggling—they looked comfortable together, like friends. Like more than friends.

Like they didn't want to be interrupted.

Adam hated himself for the tendrils of jealousy creeping through him and for the fact that he couldn't drive Kaia's mocking warnings out of his mind. He had nothing to worry about. He *knew* that. Knew that he could just say her name, or clear his throat, and they would look up and welcome him to the table, and together, they would eat cookies and slurp chocolate milk and complain about the SATs or their asshole swim coach or whatever. He could and he should, he knew that. And yet—

He didn't. He stepped backward, silently, away from them, and eased the door shut behind him. He walked a few paces down the hall, then slammed a fist into a locker in frustration. It didn't help. So he kept going, down the hall, out of the building, back home. Alone.

And inside the newspaper office, Beth looked at Kane, Kane looked at Beth, and, engrossed in the conversation, engrossed in each other, they never noticed a thing.

chapter

6

It had taken Harper about twenty-four hours to notice that Miranda wasn't speaking to her—unanswered calls, unreturned messages, a cold shoulder in the hallway and an empty seat in the cafeteria. By Tuesday night it had become pretty clear to Harper that she'd somehow screwed up. She knew it would take less than ten minutes to get Miranda—the ultimate pushover, at least when it came to Harper—to forgive her for it. Too bad she didn't have the slightest clue what "it" was.

But maybe she could bluff it out.

After countless unreturned messages ("Rand, come on, call me back—I'm sorry, I totally screwed up. Call me!"), the phone finally rang.

"Do you even know what you're apologizing for?" Miranda asked as soon as Harper picked up the phone.

Harper squirmed. Sometimes she was sorry Miranda knew her so well.

"Of course I do," she said indignantly. "And I'm sorry—I swear, I'll never do it again."

"What?"

"I said, I'll never do it again, I promise."

Miranda sucked in a sharp, exasperated breath. "No, I heard you. I mean, *what* will you never do again?"

Harper paused. "Well, I'll never do anything like *this* again, I'll tell you that much."

Miranda snorted. "You're unbelievable—you really have no idea, do you?"

Harper crumbled under the pressure. "Okay, you got me. No, I don't. But I'm sorry, I swear—just tell me what I'm supposed to be sorry about."

"Well, *if you only had a brain*, maybe you could figure it out," Miranda said cryptically.

"If I only had a—oh God, *The Wizard of Oz*. Shit, Miranda, I totally forgot!"

"Uh, yeah."

"I really am sorry." And she was. Harper wasn't a slave to tradition the way Miranda was, but she looked forward to their *Wizard of Oz* trip each year. It was a chance to blow off steam, to pretend they were kids again, to gorge themselves on candy. Plus, she had to admit . . . she really liked the movie. "I totally suck," she admitted. "Let's go tomorrow, okay?"

"Harper, it closed," Miranda said harshly. "That's kind of the point, remember? We always go on the last day. We've only been doing it for like, five years?"

"Okay, I suck. I completely and totally suck. Is this it? Are you done with me? You are, aren't you?" Harper affected a voice of exaggerated desperation. When in doubt, make 'em laugh. "You're getting rid of me and finding a new best friend. Who is it, Katie? Eloise? You know she's a shrew, so I'd advise against her. Tara? You always liked her better anyway, didn't you? And why not? I'm a horrible, terrible person. . . ."

"Quit the melodrama, Harper. You're not funny."

"Not even a little?"

She was rewarded by a muffled laugh on the other end of the phone—and Harper knew she'd got her.

"Not even a little," Miranda confirmed, unconvincingly. "In fact, you're right. You do totally suck. I should just find a new best friend." But Miranda's familiar playful sarcasm had replaced her tone of bitter anger.

"Yeah, it would probably be good for you—but when is something good for you ever any fun?" Harper asked.

"Point taken."

"So we're okay?" Harper abandoned the comedy for a second. Miranda had to know she was sincere. "I really am sorry."

"You should be—but yes, we're okay."

"I knew it. You can't live without me!"

"Don't press your luck," Miranda cautioned her. "So where were you, anyway?"

There was a pause—since she hadn't realized that she'd ditched Miranda, Harper hadn't bothered to come up with a good excuse. But what was she supposed to say, "I was out with our worst enemy, plotting a way to set up the guy you're crushing on with another girl"? In this case, it didn't seem likely that honesty would be the best policy.

"I was . . . at the dentist. It was an emergency."

"A *tooth* emergency?" Miranda asked dubiously.

"Yeah, I chipped a molar, and I managed to get the guy to see me right away. Thank God."

"It hurt a lot, huh?"

"It still does." Why had she said that? Now she was going to have to fake a toothache for the rest of the week. First rule of successful lying: Keep it simple, and never offer more information than necessary. She'd had a lot of practice.

"Must have been horrible," Miranda said sympathetically. "We're talking acute, throbbing, knives-digging-into-you pain?"

"Uh-huh." It was sort of true, if you counted the pain of having to lie to Miranda 24/7—and having to rely on Kaia, of all people.

"Brutal, agonizing pain?"

"Yeah."

Miranda laughed. "Good."

Payback came on Friday night. As the wounded party, Miranda got to pick the activity, and after a few days of careful thought, she'd settled on the perfect punishment. Karaoke. Both girls were equally averse to the torture and public humiliation that Karaoke Night at the Lasso Lounge represented, but Miranda figured it was worth sitting through an hour of off-key crooning to see Harper make a fool of herself in public. She'd been right.

"You aren't really going to make me do this," Harper complained, as a hefty man crooned Clay Aiken's latest "hit" up on the makeshift stage.

"Oh, I so am," Miranda replied with an evil laugh.

"This is cruel and unusual punishment, you know," Harper pointed out.

Miranda smiled sweetly. "What are friends for?" She pointed to the short line of would-be American Idols who had assembled by the stage. "Now get over there and show 'em what you're made of."

Harper glared at her, gulped down the last of her drink, and stalked off toward the line. "I hate you," she tossed over her shoulder.

Miranda just raised her drink in a one-sided toast. "Don't forget to smile!"

Then she leaned back in her chair and waited for the fun to start. This was going to be good.

Too many hours and too many drinks later, Harper and Miranda stumbled out of the bar on a karaoke high. Midway through her Cyndi Lauper spectacular, Harper had abandoned her embarrassment and belted out "Girls Just Wanna Have Fun" at the top of her lungs. She'd scored a round of thunderous applause and returned to the table flushed and ready for more. And after another margarita, Miranda had conceded to go with her, kicking off a marathon sing-along that took them back to the endless afternoons they'd spent as kids, choreographing dance moves to the latest on MTV. The humiliation factor was through the roof—but there was no one there to see them, and by that point in the night, they didn't even care. After a rousing, girl-power version of "I Will Survive," the karaoke machine had finally shut down, the lights went out, and Harper and Miranda were forced to seek a new adventure.

So phase two of the night was planned during the tail end of phase one, which meant that clear, sober thinking had been left far behind by the time Harper suggested they stop off for supplies.

The result of their giggly stumble through the twenty-four-hour convenience store?

A two-pound bag of Mike and Ikes (on sale for Halloween), a two-gallon bottle of Diet Coke and another of Hawaiian Punch (mixers), a six-pack of Jell-O pudding (because, well, just because—thanks to the two pitchers of margaritas back at the Lasso Lounge, they no longer needed a reason). And the pièce de résistance: a box of hair dye that promised to "change your color—and your life—in three easy steps." It was time for Miranda to become a bottle blonde.

"You said you wanted a change, right?" Harper asked, tossing the box into their shopping basket, despite Miranda's halfhearted protests.

They stumbled back to Harper's house with the goods—her parents were off in Ludlow for the weekend, visiting her great-uncle in his nursing home, a trip that Harper had easily resisted being guilted into. Great-Uncle Horace had no idea who she was and last time had insisted on referring to her as Fanny, apparently the name of a British nurse who'd been "kind" to him during the war.

Harper's parents didn't mind her staying home alone, as long as she had "that responsible Miranda" around to keep an eye on things. If they only knew.

One very messy and wet shampoo later, Miranda's hair was thoroughly coated with dye, and the two of them had nothing left to do but wait for it to dry. They fidgeted impatiently, leafing through magazines and flipping through the TV channels—Friday night was pretty much a home entertainment dead zone.

Miranda refused to look in a mirror until it was perfectly dry—she said she wanted to wait to get the full effect. And, as Harper watched with horror as Miranda's hair dried and the final color emerged, she concluded that postponing the inevitable could only be a good thing. But finally they could wait no longer.

"Okay, I can't stand it anymore," Miranda said. "How does it look?"

"Uh . . . it's different," Harper hedged. "It's definitely different."

"Well I *know* that—but how does it look? Oh, forget it. I need to see for myself."

She bounded up, but Harper leaped ahead of her and jumped in front of the mirror.

"Before you look, I just want to remind you of what you said before, how I'm such a good friend to you."

"Of course you are, Harper—this was your idea, wasn't it? I'm not going to forget that."

"That's what I'm afraid of," Harper murmured. But she stepped aside.

Miranda's scream would have woken up Harper's parents, had they been home—as it was, Harper suspected it might still have woken them up a hundred miles away in Ludlow. It might even have woken up Great-uncle Horace—and he was deaf.

"Harper—what have you done to me?" Miranda cried, lunging toward her. Harper jumped away, searching for some large piece of furniture she could put between herself and the newly psychotic Miranda.

"Don't blame me," she protested. "I followed the directions. I think." She ducked unsuccessfully as Miranda threw a pillow at her head.

"Look what you've done to me!" Miranda yelled. She slumped down on the bed and burst into—well, Harper couldn't tell whether it was sobs or hysterical laughter.

"Are you . . . okay?" Harper asked tentatively, sitting down beside her.

"Okay?" Miranda asked, tears of laughter streaming down her face. "How could I be okay? I look like Kermit the Frog!"

Sad, but true.

Miranda's rust-colored hair had been changed in three easy steps, all right—her head was now topped with a frizzy mass of bright green tendrils, the color of celery. Or of everyone's favorite Muppet.

It was horrifying. Humiliating. And hilarious.

Unable to control herself any longer, Harper burst into giggles.

Miranda fell backward onto the bed, gasping for breath. "It's not funny," she complained.

"I know," Harper said, trying to force a solemn and sober look.

"Except that it is," Miranda admitted, breaking into laughter once more.

"I know," Harper agreed, laughing again herself. She felt a rush of relief that Miranda didn't want to kill her—but she worried about what would happen in the morning, when the alcoholic glee had washed out of her system and, sober and hungover, she still looked like a Muppet. Things might not seem so jolly in the light of day.

After all, it's not easy being green.

(Just ask Kermit.)

It was Friday night, date night, and things were going to be different. Beth was determined. Adam had been acting weird all week—though she wasn't even sure what would classify as "weird" these days. Stand-offish? Short-tempered? Irritable? How was that any different, really, from the way things were the rest of the time? When was the last time they'd been together—and *talked*—without it turning into a fight? It used to be so easy to talk to Adam, and now it was just easier not to.

But tonight really would be different. Tonight would be an actual date. Not a half-rushed hookup in her bedroom before her parents got home, not a stolen few minutes between classes or a stale slice of pizza after work. Tonight it was just the two of them, all night long. And it would be fun, and easy, no matter how hard she had to work at it.

She'd suckered Adam into taking her to the Frontier Festival, an annual carnival that passed through town every October, ostensibly to celebrate the harvest (though Beth was unsure what kind of harvest a mining town, much less a defunct mining town, had to offer). Really it was just an excuse for cotton candy, funnel cake, 4-H livestock con-tests, and a rickety Ferris wheel. Beth had loved it as a child, and had always dreamed of walking through the booths and crowds of squealing children on the arm of a handsome boy. Now she finally had one.

It started out just as she'd hoped. Hand in hand, they

traipsed through the colorful booths, mocking the lame Wild West theme, squealing in fear and delight as the carnival rides swung them through the air, gorging themselves on cotton candy and corn dogs. Adam even spent ten dollars trying to win her a prize—but the water gun target shoot, the whack-a-mole, even the basketball free-throw game failed to cough up any booty. Finally Beth tried her hand at Skee-Ball, and in about five minutes had succeeded in winning Adam a stuffed pink elephant, which he accepted with a rueful but gracious grin. It was relaxing, carefree, fun, sweet—and it couldn't last.

Adam spotted him first, but Beth was the one to call him over. That was before she noticed the buxom brunette on his arm. Kane waved eagerly and hurried over to say hello, his Kewpie doll following close on his heels. In a moment everyone was introduced.

Beth, meet Hilary, a brainless idiot with a twenty-three-inch waist and a six-inch hollow space in her head.

You can't judge her before she even opens her mouth, Beth chided herself, appalled by her nasty knee-jerk reaction. She smiled at Hilary and, as sweetly as she could to make up for the evil thoughts swarming around her head, asked, "So, Hilary, do you go to Haven High too? I don't think I've ever seen you around."

Hilary giggled, and responded in a thin, airy voice. "Oh, no, I'm homeschooled—my parents think public school teaches you to be immoral."

Beth and Adam both shifted uncomfortably in silence. What, exactly, was one supposed to say to that?

No matter—Hilary wasn't waiting for an answer. She draped an arm around Kane's waist.

"Of course," she giggled again, "now I've got Kane for that. Right, sweetie?" She slapped him gently on the ass and he jumped in surprise, flashing Beth and Adam a bemused and slightly abashed look. At least, Beth read it as abashed—but maybe she was wrong, since the next thing he did was pull Hilary toward him and give her a long, hard kiss. How embarrassed by her could he be?

After a long moment he released Hilary, who looked up at him, flushed and adoring.

"I'm teaching her everything I know about bad behavior," Kane explained.

Hilary put on a fake pout and a grating baby voice. "And now I'm a bad, bad girl, aren't I?"

"You sure are," Kane agreed, pinching her ass.

"Ooh!" she squealed. "I'll get you for that." And she lunged toward him.

It was the obvious start of some kind of tickle slap fight that Beth was sure would soon end in another grope match—not something she needed to see.

"Come on, Adam," she whispered, tugging at his shirt. "Let's go."

They waved hasty good-byes and began to back away from the squealing couple.

"Off to win your lady love a bigger prize?" Kane called out from amid the tickle storm. He gestured to the small stuffed elephant Beth was holding in her arms; Hilary was toting a stuffed pink panda about four times as large.

"Actually, I won this for *him*," Beth pointed out.

"A true champion, eh?" Kane called jovially. Then his voice grew serious and he locked eyes with Beth, ignoring the giggling and pawing going on around him. "I never had any doubt."

Beth tore her gaze away with difficulty.

"Let's go," she urged Adam again. "Now."

Once they were a safe distance away, Adam began to shake with laughter.

"He's a real piece of work," he said, shaking his head.

"Him? What about *her*?" Beth asked as they wandered toward the Ferris wheel.

"Ah, she's no different from any of the other girls he picks up. Smarter, maybe."

"Smarter? You've got to be kidding me." Beth rolled her eyes and climbed into a Ferris wheel cart after Adam. They began to swing upward toward the stars.

"No, it's true—think about it, any girl with half a brain at our school is too smart to go near him."

"That's a nice way to talk about your best friend," she scolded him.

"What? He'd admit it himself—the guy's a player. Besides, you're the one always calling him a sleaze."

"That was before I got to know him."

"Trust me, Beth, if you knew him the way I do, you'd believe me. I love the guy and all, but I gotta call it like I see it." He put an arm around her shoulders and pulled her close to him, running a warm hand up and down her bare shoulders. Beth shivered, suddenly noticing the cool night air blowing past.

"How about we stop talking about Kane and his latest bimbo and just enjoy the view," Adam suggested.

"It is beautiful," Beth agreed, looking out over the glittering sprawl beneath them. A range of low-slung mountains loomed in the distance, silhouetted by the full moon.

They sat quietly for a moment until Beth couldn't take it anymore—the words boiled up inside of her and finally leaked out.

"I just don't see why he does it!" she exclaimed, flinging her arms up for emphasis.

"Who?"

"Kane—he's so much better than these girls."

"Why are you getting so angry?" Adam asked in frustrated confusion. "What do you care?"

"I just—I just want him to be happy. Don't you? He's *your* friend."

"That's right, he's *my* friend," he repeated. "And I can tell you that he *is* happy. I'm the one sitting up here while my girlfriend goes crazy over another guy. Too jealous of Kane to care whether I'm happy?"

"I am *not* jealous," Beth protested indignantly.

"Whatever."

"I just think he's a great guy," she insisted. "He deserves better."

"Like who? You?"

"Stop it, Adam," she said irritably. "If you don't want to talk about him anymore, we won't talk about him anymore. You don't have to make such a big deal about it."

He crossed his arms and peered out over the side, away from her. "Fine."

"Fine."

And so they didn't talk at all.

Kaia knew things. It was second nature now, after her long years of training—part skill, part talent, whatever. Everyone needs a hobby. In New York, after all those years with the same people, the same streets, the same hangouts, it had been easy. You just had to listen, ask the right questions, be in the right place at the right time, learn how to be invisible. This last, for Kaia, had been the hardest lesson to learn, as she'd made a life out of being seen, being *noticed*—but it turned out that didn't always serve her purposes. Knowledge was power, and when you were a teenager, held hostage by the arbitrary whims of adults who mistakenly thought they knew best, you needed all the power you could get.

After sifting through the skeletons in the closets of half of the Upper West Side, the denizens of Grace, California, didn't really pose much trouble for Kaia's investigative skills, especially since, at the moment, she had very little else to do. So even though she'd been in town for only a month, she knew things, big and small.

She knew that the servants played poker together in the room above the garage every Sunday night—and that their drink supplies always came courtesy of the Sellers family liquor cabinet. She knew that Alicia, the married maid, was screwing Howard, Kaia's father's driver. She knew that the Haven High principal was having an affair with her English teacher, that Adam's mother was well deserving of her reputation as the town slut, that her gym teacher was an alcoholic kleptomaniac, that her middle-aged mailman was still emotionally debilitated by the tragic loss of his mother in 1987, and that the woman who ran the local post office was a thirty-seven-year-old virgin. Of course she knew about Harper's and Kane's little crushes—that was child's play.

And she knew that every Friday night from eight p.m. to closing, the bar stool on the far left in the Prairie Dog Bar and Grill was occupied by one Mr. Jack Powell.

Yes, knowing things could come in handy.

It was a hole in the wall, with room for no more than ten customers at once (though crowding was never a problem). The grill, if it had ever truly existed, must have broken long ago, for the only food available was the stale peanut and pretzel mix filling the spotted beer mugs spread across the bar, and the moldy cheese left as bait in the mousetraps in the corners. Other than the bartender, a smiling old man with no hair and plenty of rounded edges, Jack Powell was the only one there.

She sidled up to the bar and hopped onto the stool next to him. He was hunched over a mug of beer, reading a book. *No Exit*, by Sartre. How appropriate.

"Kind of a bleak choice for Friday night," she observed, peering over his shoulder at the tiny print.

He looked up in horror and practically fell off his stool at the sight of her.

"Are you stalking me now?" he asked drily, regaining his composure as she laughed in his face.

"Please—you should be so lucky. I'm here for a drink and some peace and quiet, just like you."

"And until a moment ago I thought I'd found it," he grumbled.

"Can I get a Corona?" she called to the bartender, ignoring Powell.

"Don't serve her," Powell instructed him. "She's under age."

The bartender winked. "Hey, buddy, I won't tell if you

won't." He slid a bottle down the bar toward Kaia. "On the house, beautiful."

"You must be pretty used to getting exactly what you want," Powell said in disgust.

"Pretty much," she agreed.

"You're fighting a losing battle this time."

"You think this is me fighting?" She shook her head. He could be so cute when he was being clueless. "Please— this is me on low gear, getting a drink. It's just good luck we two lonely hearts happened to run into each other."

"And you just happened to be wearing . . . practically nothing?" he asked sardonically, gesturing toward her barely-there silk top.

"So you noticed," she said with pleasure, running her fingers lightly along her bare breastbone. "And here I thought it was just my imagination, your staring at my chest all the time."

"It's a bit difficult not to, with your shoving it in my face like that."

"Jack, Jack, Jack." She shook her head ruefully. "You can insult me all you want. I'm not leaving."

"No, but I am." He closed his book and stood up, slapping a ten-dollar bill down on the bar. "Thanks, Joey," he called to the bartender.

"And where will you go?" Kaia asked. "Home? To sit alone in your pathetic little bachelor pad until you can force yourself to go to sleep? Or maybe to the library— would that be more your speed?"

"I'll be quite happy to go anywhere you're not," he informed her. "Thanks for ruining my night."

"I'm the best part of your night, and you know it. Or

were you having more fun a few minutes ago, sitting here alone in this cellar, mooning over your beer like a drunken poet?"

"Fun doesn't seem to be in my vocabulary these days," he admitted with a dispirited sigh. "This isn't the town for it."

"You're just not looking hard enough, Mr. Powell." She put her finger softly to his lips and raised her other hand to his temple—and for once, she noticed, he didn't twist away. "Stop talking, for once, and open your eyes."

He raised his hands and gently removed hers from his face. But he let them linger in his grasp for a moment too long, and it was she who broke contact first—but not before raising one of his hands to her lips and grazing his knuckles with a gentle kiss.

He pulled away quickly.

"I'm seeing things pretty clearly right now," he said sharply. "And I can see that it's time for me to go." He slipped out of the bar and Kaia sat down again, sipping her Corona thoughtfully.

He could run—but he couldn't hide.

Kaia would always know where to find him.

It seemed the farther they got from the festival—and from Kane—the better things were. By the time they got back to Adam's house, Beth was smiling, a look of glazed contentedness on her face. Maybe it was just the slow descent from a cotton candy sugar high—but whatever the reason, Adam thought as she snuggled close to him, he'd take it.

"It's such a nice night," she said, taking his hand as she climbed out of the car. "I almost hate to go inside."

He checked his watch. There was only an hour left before her curfew, not enough time to go anywhere, but . . .

"How about we go around back," he suggested. He led her into the backyard and over to the large, flat rock that lay on the dividing line between his house and Harper's. He and Harper had played there when they were little and always—even these days—considered it "their" place. He snuck a guilty glance up at Harper's bedroom window, which overlooked the yard. She wouldn't mind—she would, in fact, never know.

Beth clambered up atop the rock and lay back on it, spreading her arms and looking up at the clear, starry sky.

"You could lose yourself in the stars," she sighed. "Out here, in the dark, you could forget the whole world, and just—be."

"I know exactly what you mean," Adam said, lying down next to her. "I could lose myself in you." He took her face in his hands and turned it toward him gently, kissing her forehead, her nose, her cheeks, her soft, smooth lips. She brushed her blond hair away from her face and pulled him closer to her, tangling her legs in his. The smooth rock surface was cool beneath his skin, but she was so warm, throbbing with heat as she grazed the lines of his body and began to rub the bare skin beneath his shirt.

"I'm sorry I was so . . . I'm sorry about tonight," she murmured.

"It was nothing. Forget it," he assured her, cradling her in his arms.

"I'm just stressed—there's so much to do, and no time, and—"

"Shh." She was trembling in his arms, and he put his hand to her cheek, then ran his fingers across her lips. "It's okay. I know. It'll be okay."

"I miss you," she whispered.

"We just need to make it through the SATs," he suggested. "And then maybe you can take a break for a while. We can take a break, focus on us. No stress, no SATs, no homework. Just us."

"It sounds perfect," Beth sighed. "I can't wait." She lay her head on his chest. "I could just lie here forever, listening to you breathe."

He ran his fingers through her hair and began softly massaging her back, rubbing and kneading her taut muscles, her tender skin.

"I wish you could," he whispered. "Next week. Just keep telling yourself that. You'll make it until then. *We'll* make it until then."

"I hope so," she whispered.

So did he.

chapter

7

"No way in hell am I going out in public looking like this," Miranda wailed.

As Harper had expected, Miranda had awoken with a raging hangover and a far stormier outlook on being a green-headed monster.

"Well, on the bright side . . . ," Harper began.

"I don't want to hear it," Miranda interrupted her. "It's too early in the morning for bright sides."

"It's twelve thirty," Harper pointed out. They'd rolled out of bed a few minutes ago and were now slouched in front of the kitchen table, trying to cure their hangover with juice and a handful of aspirin.

"Am I in my pajamas? Am I eating Rice Krispies? Am I still waiting for my first cup of coffee? Then it's morning."

Harper, whose own head was throbbing with the pain of one margarita too many, was in no position to argue.

"Look, we'll fix this," she promised.

"You'd better," Miranda growled. "It's your fault I look like the Jolly Green Midget to begin with."

"We'll take care of it, I promise. The box said it washes out in twenty to twenty-five shampoos, right? So all we need to do is wash your hair twenty-five times in a row, and that should be that."

"That's a lot of showers. . . ."

"Do you *want* to go to school on Monday looking like a stalk of broccoli?" Harper asked wryly.

Miranda looked appalled at the thought. "Hey, it's not like we're in the middle of a drought or anything," she said, reconsidering. "Bring on the shampoo."

"Uh, actually, we're going to need to go get some more of that," Harper reminded her. They'd used the last of it the night before in their drunken beauty school efforts. But perhaps the less said about that, the better.

"We?" Miranda squawked. "Did I mention that I am *not* going out in public like this? Which part of that did you not understand?"

"Chill out—I'll go to the drugstore and get more shampoo. Just let me throw on some clothes."

"Fine," Miranda sulked. "I'll jump in the shower. Might as well get started."

The two of them scampered upstairs, Harper to hastily throw on some clothes and Miranda to single-handedly bring on a drought. As she pulled on a T-shirt, Harper idly picked up her cell phone and noticed she had a text message waiting for her from Kane. *1:37, elementary school playground. Be there. Bring Adam.*

Cryptic much? Harper thought grouchily. It was definitely too early in the morning for riddles.

She called Kane immediately.

"What are you talking about?" she asked, without saying hello.

"Can't talk now—*Beth* and I are studying," he said meaningfully. "Just trust me—you won't want to miss this."

"But what—?"

"Can't *talk* now," he repeated. "Just be on time."

He hung up, and Harper sighed, casting a glance toward the bathroom door, where the water in the shower had just turned off.

"When you're out getting the shampoo, can you grab us some lunch, too?" Miranda called from behind the door.

Harper cradled her head in her hands. Really, what was she supposed to do? Jeopardize the whole plan just because Miranda was having a hair crisis? It wasn't even a tough call—she'd just need to come up with a good excuse.

"Rand, change of plans—I'm going to need to run you home," she said casually.

Miranda swung open the door and popped out, towel hastily wrapped around her dripping body.

"What? I must have heard you wrong, because I thought you said you were abandoning me."

"Rand—"

"But that can't be right. Not you, my best friend, who just ditched me five days ago and promised never to do it again and who—"

"Rand—," Harper helplessly tried again.

"*Who*, by the way, turned my hair *green*!" She grabbed some clothes and went back into the bathroom, slamming the door behind her. "So, lunch," she said. "I'm thinking pizza? Or Chinese food?"

"Stop acting like a baby, Miranda. I have to take a rain check. It's an emergency."

Harper waited in silence for several minutes, until finally a fully dressed—though still dripping—Miranda emerged from the bathroom.

"What kind of emergency?" she asked suspiciously.

"Well, not an emergency exactly—I mean, it's not life threatening," Harper hedged, thinking fast. "It's just, you remember that tooth problem I was having? That was the dentist on the phone—he says he can fit me in for a follow-up, but only if I come right away. Some kind of last-minute cancellation."

"Follow-up?"

"Yeah, my tooth is still killing me." Harper brought one hand to her jaw, hoping that Miranda wouldn't remember which side of her mouth the fake toothache was supposed to be on, since Harper no longer had any idea. "Of course, if you really need me, I guess I could just suffer through the pain. . . ."

Miranda heaved an exaggerated sigh.

"No, I can take a shower—or thirty of them—all by myself. I'm a big girl, after all."

"I'll come over tonight and we'll do final damage control, I promise."

"I can't wait to see the look on my mother's face when she sees this one," Miranda said with a sudden smile. "You know, it'll almost be worth it."

"You see? There's a silver lining after all."

Miranda shot Harper her patented Look of Death. "I said, *almost.*"

✧✧✧

"It's such a beautiful day," Kane had mused. "Why don't we do this study thing outside?"

Beth had reluctantly agreed. It's not that she didn't want to go outside—in fact, on a day like this, with a light breeze blowing and only a few wispy clouds in the sky, the last thing she wanted to do was sit inside and stare at fractions. But they had a lot to get through, and not much time. Being outside would be a distraction.

It was just so hard to say no to him.

They ended up in the playground of their old elementary school, stretched out on a picnic blanket between the swings and the jungle gym. The playground served as a park on the weekends, and laughing children swarmed all around them.

Still, Kane stayed focused. More focused even than Beth, who kept looking around at the playground equipment with something akin to longing. She came here by herself sometimes, at dusk, to sit on the swings and watch the sunset. It was a good place to think—surrounded by memories of a simpler time, all those games of tag and four square, the races she'd run, the games she'd lost and won, the swings she'd been on constantly, whooshing through the air as if she could fly.

She'd be going to college in a year, and there were very few parts of the town that she'd be sorry to see go. She'd been born here, grown up here, knew it inside and out. There were a few people she never wanted to leave behind—Adam, of course, her family, and—she looked at Kane—new friends too, the ones she'd missed getting to know all these years. But the town itself? She was ready to leave Grace in the past, never to be seen again. All except the playground. It was a special place. *Her* place.

And really, it was all that remained of her childhood.

Kane yawned and stretched himself out on the picnic blanket, preening in the sun like a lazy and self-satisfied cat.

"Late night last night?" Beth asked sarcastically, trying her best not to admire his impeccable physique.

"I know, I know, Heather's a little—"

"Hilary," Beth corrected him.

"What?"

"Her name was *Hilary,*" she reminded him with a reproachful glare.

Kane at least had the grace to blush.

"Ah, yeah. Hilary's a little—well, she's not like you. She's just . . . fun."

"So I'm not fun?" *Why do I even care what he thinks of me?* she asked herself.

"You're fun and so much more, Manning," he said languidly.

"And that means what, exactly?"

"It means you're cute when you're mad—anyone ever tell you that?"

"You're changing the subject," she pointed out, ignoring the compliment. That was just the kind of thing Kane said, after all, she reminded herself. Just the kind of guy he was. It didn't mean anything.

Kane sighed. "It means that you're fun, but that's not all there is. Girls like Heather—"

"Hilary."

"Whatever—they're a dime a dozen," he explained. "Girls like you? There aren't so many."

Now it was Beth who blushed. "I just hate to see you wasting your time, Kane. You deserve so much more."

"I can't believe this is coming from you, of all people."

"Why me, 'of all people'?"

"Come on, Beth," he said, looking away. "I know how girls like you see me. You think I'm a sleazy flirt. Not worth your time. Girls like you think I'm worthless."

"Not all of us," she murmured.

"What?"

She was suddenly struck by the unusual sincerity, the urgency in his voice. And she didn't like it.

"Let's just—uh—let's get back to work," she suggested, bending back over her notebook. "So, when the exponent is in the denominator, you want to . . ."

The problem was, she didn't know *how* she saw him anymore—but she suspected it was time to stop looking.

Adam had been surprised when Harper called suggesting they take a walk down to the old playground. Reminiscing about the past wasn't usually her thing—Harper was all about living in the moment.

But neither of them had anything better to do, and it couldn't hurt to go visit the site of some of their best exploits. Just because Beth was off somewhere studying with Kane, *again*, didn't mean he needed to sit around the house all day sulking. He needed to take his mind off of things—and no one did that better than Harper.

"Why do you keep checking your cell every five minutes?" he asked her, just after pointing out the spot where Danny Burger, fifth-grade stud, had wet his pants. In fear of ruining his too-cool-for-school rep, he'd promised the witnesses three packs of baseball cards each in return for their eternal silence—and then run the whole two miles back to his house. "Are you expecting a call?"

"No, I left my watch at home and I just want to see what time it is—I have a dentist appointment later. Let's walk a little faster," she suggested.

As they reached the gate of the small playground, Harper pointed toward a couple by the swings.

"Isn't that Beth? And Kane?" she asked.

Adam squinted at the couple—it was them, all right. Kane was pushing Beth higher and higher, and he could imagine the exuberant look on her face as she stretched her toes closer and closer to the sky. He'd seen it enough times himself.

Harper raised a hand to wave, but he grabbed it and stopped her.

"No, let's just—just wait, okay?"

She gave him a cryptic look, but shrugged in agreement. So they just stood at the fence and watched.

"What are they doing here, anyway?" Harper asked. "I thought they were studying."

Adam's stomach clenched. "Yeah, so did I."

"We should really get back to work now," Beth complained, breathless with exertion.

Kane checked his watch. One thirty-five.

Harper had better be out there somewhere, he thought.

It was the perfect setup—the picnic, the romantic frolicking on the swings. And that whole heart-to-heart on his dating life? Talk about an unexpected pleasure. So Beth was paying attention, was she? He'd been unsure of how to play it last night—too much macho pig with all the leering and groping? Would it erode all the hard work he'd put into changing her image of him?

But as soon as he'd seen the look on her face, he'd known he had her. She was disgusted, sure—but she also, for a split second, wanted to *be* Hilary, wanted to forget all her uptight, repressed, do-gooder rules and restrictions and just fall into his arms. It was a look he'd recognize anywhere.

One thirty-seven. Time for the coup de grâce.

"Just a couple more minutes, sarge?" he grinned down at her—and, surprise, surprise, she couldn't resist. "Just once down the slide," he suggested.

"Okay," she conceded. "But you first."

Perfect.

He slid down, waving as he went and then tapped her lightly on the shoulder. "Your turn, teach."

She climbed up the narrow ladder and stood paused at the top, looking down at him dubiously.

"This is a little higher than I remember," she said nervously.

"What are you, chicken?" he called up to her. "Five-year-olds slide down this thing. Don't worry, I'll be down here at the bottom to catch you."

He waited for her, and watched as she slid down the rusty and pitted metal, her blond hair cascading behind her, a grin of delight illuminating her flushed and open face. Kane had been with a lot of girls, but he'd never known any who could be made so happy by so little. In fact, he usually ran a little more toward the high maintenance end of the spectrum, girls who could accept a gold bracelet with an upturned nose and a faint "Thanks, I guess." But Beth—he shook his head in bemusement. Give her a freshly baked chocolate chip cookie, swing her through the air, it would be enough. She'd be happy. And it was real happiness, the kind that spills over its borders, pours into everyone around you. *That* he'd never seen before.

She slid with a squeal into his arms, and the momentum knocked them both backward onto the scraggly bed of grass, where they lay tangled in each other's arms, heaving with laughter. For a moment Kane even forgot why he was there, what he was doing, who was watching.

Then he remembered—and felt a sudden stab of an emotion so unfamiliar he barely recognized it: guilt.

Adam stood motionless, his face impassive, carved in stone.

Harper reached a tentative hand out toward him.

"Adam, I'm sure it's just—"

"Don't, Harper. Just—don't."

He was clenching the chain link fence so hard that his knuckles turned white, and Harper could see a small muscle twitching just above his jawline—but those were the only exterior signs of whatever was churning within him at the sight of Beth and Kane rolling around on the ground in each other's arms.

"I'm sure it's nothing," he said quietly. "They're just taking a break. Nothing wrong with that."

Harper stayed silent, waiting for him to give her some sign of what to do next. Finally he pulled himself away from the fence, turned his back on the playground.

"Let's go," he said shortly. "Let's just go."

Harper hated to see Adam in pain, much less to know

that she was the one responsible for it—but in this case . . . well, wasn't it better for him to suffer a little pain now, if it would help him avoid a much greater pain later on, when he finally realized on his own that Beth was the wrong girl? Or when *she* left *him*, for college or for another guy or for no reason at all? *Just look at her,* Harper thought in disgust. Running around with Kane, throwing herself into his arms. The timing might have been a trick, but what they were looking at? That was real. That was betrayal.

And when you looked at it that way, she was doing Adam a favor. Just helping a good friend see the light.

Miranda had snuck into her house as quietly as she could.

It wasn't quietly enough.

At the sound of the door her mother came clattering down the stairs and, after a horrified tirade on the state of Miranda's head, let loose with the bad news: She needed some peace and quiet. Which meant she was sending Miranda's little sister, Stacy, to the Frontier Festival—in care of Miranda.

And she wouldn't take "No way in hell am I leaving the house like this" for an answer.

The festival turned out to be just as bad as she'd expected. Hokey and crowded, it would have been pun-ishment enough on its own—but with green hair? It was torture. Everywhere they went, Miranda felt like people were staring at her (perhaps because Stacy kept pointing at her head and shouting, "My sister has green hair!"). *They might as well put me in the freak show,* she thought drily. *Come one, come all, see the Amazing Human Chia Pet.*

"Hey, it's the mean, green, fighting machine!" One of

the barkers suddenly called out. "Where are you going?"

She looked around. The screechy voice booming from the megaphone could only be coming from the tall, gawky boy manning a dunk booth—and it could only be directed toward Miranda.

She shook it off. *Just keep walking,* she told herself.

"Come on, show us your stuff, Incredible Hulk style!" he called. "Three throws for a dollar—I dare you."

"Randa, he's talking to you," Stacy pointed out, eyes wide. As if she hadn't noticed.

"Forget it, Stacy. We're leaving."

"But—"

"What are you, scared? Where are you hiding your wings, chicken?" When he started clucking, that was it. Enough was enough. Miranda heaved a huge sigh and turned her sister back around.

"Come on, Stacy, it's time to dunk a dunce."

The annoying barker—a tall, skinny teen with glasses and a striped T-shirt that made him look like a live action Where's Waldo—grinned and collected their money, then scrambled up onto a wooden bench that hovered precariously over the tank of water. He waved cheerfully.

"Worried?" Miranda asked as her sister readied herself to take a throw at the bull's-eye target.

"Nah—how about you?" He snickered. "You're looking a little green in the gills there."

As the loser cackled to himself, Miranda leaned down to Stacy and encouraged her.

"Throw hard, sweetie—as hard as you can."

Ball one.

Miss!

"Nice try, ladies. I'm shaking in my moccasins."

Moccasins. She should have figured. This guy had loser written all over him.

Ball two.

Miss!

"One more shot—but you're winners either way."

"You'll give her a prize even if she doesn't hit the target?" Miranda asked, pleasantly surprised.

"No, of course not—but don't you feel like you've won just by meeting me?"

"Won what?"

"The game of life, of course."

"Only if you're the booby prize," Miranda muttered. She grabbed the last ball from Stacy's hands. "Let me take this one, Stace."

Ball three.

Crack!

Splash!

Miranda and Stacy burst into uncontrollable laughter as the annoying loser flailed wildly in the shallow water, finally popping up for air.

"You think that's funny, do you?"

"Hilarious," Miranda agreed.

"Well, just remember you said that."

Before Miranda could figure out what he was talking about, he climbed out, soaking wet, and slammed his palm into a bright red panel by the tank.

"Better hold your nose," he suggested cheerfully.

Too late.

A bucket overturned over Miranda's head, unleashing a flood of icy water.

"What the hell!" she screamed, looking down at herself, post–tidal wave. Her clothes were soaked and sticking to her body, marred by a few light green streaks—apparently her hair was still water soluble.

"Language, language," water boy cautioned her with a smirk, pointing toward Stacy. "There are children here, you know." He grabbed a giant stuffed bear off the rack and handed it to the girl.

"Here you go, sweetie. Good job." He turned to Miranda. "And you."

"I get a prize too?" she asked, holding her arms out from her sides in a pathetic attempt to air dry. "I think you've already given me enough."

"You get the best prize of all." He scrawled something on a piece of paper and handed it to her.

She uncrumpled it and looked uncomprehendingly at what he'd written: "Greg—555-6733."

"My phone number," he explained, a bright red blush spreading across his face and out to the tips of his oversize ears.

"Wha—?"

"I think your hair's cute," he spit out, eyes darting away in embarrassment. "And so are you."

Kaia shut off the TV in frustration. There were only so many hours of nothing on that she could take. But what else was she supposed to do? She'd read a book, read the latest issue of *InStyle*—twice—even done her homework (truly a move of last resort). And it was still only Saturday night. She'd pretty much burned her bridges for what passed as A list social life around here, and she didn't have much interest in palling around with social climbers who thought that hanging with someone who used to be at the top of a social ladder was the next best thing to ever being there themselves. And what did that leave? Kaia, alone and bored in her father's palatial monstrosity of a midlife crisis (complete with pool table, hot tub, giant flat screen TV). After a few weeks trapped in small-town hell, even the luxury oasis wasn't cutting it.

She wondered what was going on back at the home front. Kaia got an e-mail or two a week from members of her old crowd (even, once in a while, a note from her mother, complaining about the decorator's incompetence or her dermatologist's too frequent vacations). But that was about it.

Principle dictated that she wait for them to call her and describe how empty life was without Kaia. Boredom dictated that she call them and torture herself with the knowledge of the life she should be living.

Boredom—and masochism—won out.

"Kaia, we miss you so much!" Alexa fawned. (They had all fawned over her, back in New York, jockeying for favor as if hoping her light would shine down on them and redeem their pitiful lives. It was a horrible way to think about your friends—but then, Alexa and the rest weren't *really* friends, were they? So what did it matter?) "K, you missed the sale of the season yesterday. Bergdorf's—you would not *believe* the scene."

"Oh, I can imagine."

"I should have snagged you something, but it was just too crazy."

"Well, not much call for Marc Jacobs out here in the sticks, anyway," Kaia admitted.

"Oh, that's right," Alexa said, her voice dripping with pity. "Burlap sack is maybe more your speed these days, right?" A beat. "Just kidding, of course."

"Of course," Kaia said drily.

"How are the hotties out there? You climbed into bed with any cowboys yet?"

"A few. It's slim pickings, though. Like Presley Prep on a Monday morning." Showing up in homeroom at eight a.m. on a Monday, sans hangover, was basically admitting to the world that you'd spent the weekend poring over your stamp collection. Or, Kaia thought, looking around in self-pity, forming a permanent body-size lump in your couch, flipping aimlessly through the TV channels 24/7.

"Tell me about it," Alexa drawled. "But by Tuesday— totally yummy. Tyler was getting so jealous the other day when—"

"Tyler?" *Her* Tyler? Six-feet-two Kenneth Cole addict with a nasty sense of humor and a silver Ferrari?

"Uh, yeah," Alexa mumbled. "You know we've been seeing each other. You know, nothing serious."

"I *don't* know," Kaia corrected her coolly. "Maybe you should enlighten me."

"Oh, I already told you all about it. I'm sure of it. You remember—you said you didn't care?"

It was an utter lie. But pointing that out would violate the code, the code that forbade you to ever admit to caring. Not when you were with a guy, not when the guy moved on to someone else, not when your supposed friends stabbed you in the back.

Kaia didn't really care about the code—but then again, she didn't much care about Tyler or Alexa, either. So she let it pass.

"Actually, he's here right now," Alexa finally remembered to mention. "Want to say hello? Ooh, Tyler, quit it. I'm on the phone." There was a series of giggles, then a disconcerting pause during which Alexa and her Harvard-bound hottie were doing who knows what, then, "Sorry, I'm back, what were you saying?"

Before Kaia could answer, the doorbell rang—it was like a gift from the gods.

Or possibly the delivery guy, waiting outside with the pizza she'd ordered. Either way, it was a sign.

"I was saying I have to go—hot party to get to," Kaia lied easily.

"Sure, sure—awesome to talk to you, K, we miss you so much here. Oh, Tyler, for fuck's sake, quit it. We think about you all the time. No, Tyler, I'm not talking to you, I'm talking to Kaia. *Kaia.* Tyler, stop it! I mean it!"

"Yeah, miss you, too," Kaia said dully, her voice drowned out by giggles. She shook her head in disgust and hung up the phone.

Think about her all the time? Yeah, right.

She hated them all for a moment—her parents for forcing her into exile, the friends who'd left her behind even though she was the one who'd left, Harper and her cronies here, who had all the social capital that Kaia had worked so hard to accumulate in her old life. You can't take it with you, they say.

Ain't it the truth.

She shuffled down to the front door to collect her pizza and got another unpleasant surprise.

"It's you," the scruffy delivery guy grunted when she opened the door.

"Do I know you?" It seemed a highly unlikely—and highly disturbing—prospect.

"We've met. I rescued you?" He spoke slowly, his words spaced out as if he were in danger of forgetting which one came next. It was the kind of voice that you imagined saying "yo" or "dude" every other word—so much so that the words almost didn't need to be said. They were just implied.

Still, it was true, they'd met before. Under the dweebish Guido's hat and apron was the same grody guy she and Harper had blown off in the Cactus Cantina. *And now my night is officially complete,* she thought in disgust.

"Oh yeah," she grudgingly admitted. "What was your name? Weed? Seed?"

"Reed," he corrected her, glowering. "Hopefully next time you'll get it right."

Weed would have been more appropriate, she decided, judging from the smell hovering around him and the glassy look in his eyes. He reeked of pot.

"Hopefully there won't be a next time," she retorted.

"Fine with me, princess."

"I hope you don't treat all the people you *serve* in this manner," Kaia said haughtily.

"Not too many people home to serve on a Saturday night," he said with a sly smile.

Was *he* actually criticizing *her* social life? Or would that be giving him too much credit? Veiled insults take brain power, and Kaia was sure this guy was running on empty. She knew she should just shut the door and go back to her night, lame as it was—but there was something about this guy that held her in place. Maybe it was his deep, dark, intense gaze, or the way his soft lips curled up into a knowing smile—

She shuddered. Surely she hadn't sunk low enough to be attracted to a guy like *this*. Raw sex appeal notwithstanding, he was still a delinquent pothead. A delivery boy, she reminded herself. That was it.

"Better sitting at home eating shitty pizza than running around town *delivering* it like a servant on wheels," she pointed out, trying not to watch the way his body moved beneath his tight black T-shirt.

"Dude, at least I get paid," he countered. "If you think about it, you're kind of paying me to hang out with you." He snorted and shook his head, as if pitying her. "I can think of better ways to spend my money."

"You know what? Me too." She snatched back the couple dollar bills she'd given him for a tip and slammed the door in his face.

"And then he asked you out?" In her excitement, Harper almost dropped the phone. She flopped back onto her bed and kicked her legs in the air in triumph. This could be just the loophole she was looking for.

"He gave me his phone number," Miranda clarified. "It's not the same thing."

Details, details. "Okay, but he basically asked you out. Excellent."

"Um, were you not paying attention when I described what an annoying loser he was?" Miranda asked. "And did you miss the part where he dumped a bucket of water on my head?"

"Methinks the lady doth protest too much," Harper teased her. "Besides, that was just his way of flirting. Maybe he's a little shy and awkward. I think it's adorable."

"Since when do *you* find shy and awkward adorable?"

Harper's mind was racing. Sure, *now* she was betraying Miranda by helping Kane get another girl—if you wanted to look at it that way. But as Harper saw things, Kane had made it painfully clear that he wasn't interested. Just because she'd sworn a solemn oath to Miranda that she'd do everything she could to make it happen . . . well, what was she? A magician? It's not like she had any power over what Kane wanted.

The problem was just that Miranda might not see it that way. So if Miranda found some other guy to lust over in the meantime, someone who actually wanted her in return, and she got swept up in some torrid new romance? Well, she'd stop feeling so shitty about the Kane thing and Harper could stop feeling so guilty.

Problem solved.

"I say you go for it," Harper urged. "How long has it been since you've gone out on a date?"

"Can I plead the fifth?"

"Miranda," she said warningly.

Miranda sighed. "Okay, okay, too long."

"And why is that?"

"I don't know—because I'm fat? Because I have frizzy hair that now looks vaguely like seaweed? Because I'm so short that a guy has to fall over me before he notices I exist?"

"Shut up, loser," Harper snorted. "You know none of those things are true. Plenty of guys ask you out."

"Sucky guys."

"That's exactly what I'm talking about—you're too picky. They can't *all* suck."

"Oh, trust me—"

"No, I don't trust you. You've got these impossibly high standards that no guy could ever measure up to and then you complain about being alone. I'm tired of it."

"So I'm supposed to have *no* standards?" Miranda asked.

"No, you're just supposed to be realistic. To take a chance once in a while on someone who's not one hundred percent perfect."

"I don't think Kane's perfect—"

Harper rolled her eyes, glad Miranda couldn't see her through the phone. This was getting pathetic.

"Great. So there's *one* guy in all these years who measures up. You think maybe it's time to branch out a little?"

"Why are you yelling at me?" Miranda asked in a small voice.

"I'm sorry." Harper took a deep breath. "I'm not yelling. I just want you to be happy, Rand. So what if this guy's not the one? So what if he's not as hot or as charming as the Great and Powerful Kane? You don't have to marry him—just go out with him a couple times. Think of it as practice. And who knows," she continued, hating herself for it, "maybe you'll even make Kane jealous. You know guys always want what they can't have." She knew that was one idea Miranda would find impossible to resist.

"Okay . . . you got me. I'll do it. I'll call Greg and ask him to dinner."

"Fabulous." Harper grinned and looked out her window toward Adam's bedroom. She wondered what he was thinking about right now. Probably Beth. But even that wasn't enough to deflate her mood. "Good luck, not that you need it."

Miranda sighed.

"Thanks for the reality check, Harper. You're the best."

Harper hung up the phone and gave herself a mental pat on the back for a job extremely well done. Miranda would be distracted (and, as an added bonus, maybe even happy), leaving Harper free and clear to pursue her own agenda. Guilt free.

Was Harper the best?

Damn right.

Beth slammed her hand on the dining room table as another paper airplane whizzed past her head.

"Adam, give it a rest, I'm trying to concentrate."

"Okay, okay." He bent down over his book again and there was a moment of blessed silence. But then, just when Beth had almost wrapped her head around the variables in a monstrously complicated word problem, a tiny ball of paper flew onto her book. When she looked up in irritation, another one hit her squarely in the forehead.

"Jesus, Adam, what are you, twelve years old?"

"What? I'm just trying to have some fun. You can't tell me you're not bored out of your mind."

"That's not the point," she snapped. "The SATs are in less than two weeks, and I *need* to get through this. I thought you did too—isn't that what you said?"

Actually, Adam had called to report his latest swimming victory, suggesting they go out on the town to celebrate. It was a huge moment for him—the swim team was going to the regional championships for the first time in a decade, and it was all thanks to Adam. Beth would have liked nothing more than to spend the night celebrating, to enjoy the fact that she was in love with such an amazing guy. But . . . she just didn't have the time. She'd set aside the night for SAT studying, and she couldn't break her schedule. Not this close to the test. Not even for Adam. But when she'd told him that, he hadn't gotten angry, or sulky, or any of the other reactions she'd expected. Instead, he'd invited himself over. A study date, just the two of them.

"I need to study," she'd warned him, wary that she'd be too distracted by his charming smile and silky blond hair.

"Hey, I'm taking the test too," he'd pointed out. "Don't I need to study?"

She'd been skeptical—but, after all, she'd been begging him all along to take the SATs more seriously. Who was she to object when he finally took her advice?

They had set up shop at the dining room table and, after a couple minutes of small talk, lowered their heads over their books.

For about five minutes. And then his attention span ran out.

The last hour had been insanely frustrating, as she tried to keep her concentration and her temper. But she wasn't having much luck with either.

"I just thought we could take a little break," he whined, squirming under her disapproving gaze. "Have a little fun."

"There's no time for fun—not now," Beth said, gesturing at the intimidating piles of books, notebooks, and flashcards that lay scattered across the table. She hated the way she sounded, like such a humorless stick in the mud. But it was partly his fault—if he wasn't always such a baby, she wouldn't always have to be such a nag. It's not like she enjoyed playing the role. "Why can't you understand that?"

"Maybe because you seem to have plenty of time when it comes to Kane," he said sulkily.

"Is that what this is all about? Is that why you're here?" Beth sighed in exasperation. How had Adam gotten so disconnected from the things that really mattered to her, enough so that he couldn't understand the most important things in her life? Instead, they just had to have this same pointless conversation over and over again. Maybe that was what happened when you stopped talking, she thought sadly. You ran out of new things to say. "Are you really that jealous?"

"I'm not jealous at all," he said hotly. "I just don't understand what the deal is with the two of you."

"I told you—he cares about doing well," Beth insisted. "He *wants* my help."

"That's not all he wants," Adam muttered.

"What was that?" she asked sharply.

"I just think you need to ask yourself why he wants to spend so much time with you. Why are you so sure that he cares so much about the *test*?"

She stiffened—it infuriated her when he implied that the only thing she had to offer the world was her body. Why was he so convinced that all anyone could ever want from her was sex? Maybe because it was all *he* wanted? As always, she tried to suppress the fear—but these days, it never disappeared for long.

"Oh, I don't know—maybe because when I study with *Kane*, he actually works hard," she pointed out, and it was absolutely true. "He doesn't sit there fidgeting, throwing paper airplanes, and ignoring everything I say unless it's about football or TV. Now . . . who does that sound like to you?"

"Fine!" he said in a loud, sulky voice, looking away. "You caught me. I don't give a shit about this stupid test. I just wanted to spend some time with my girlfriend. Lock me up and throw away the key."

She shushed him and glanced down the hall—her mother was trying to sleep a bit before working a night shift, and the last thing Beth needed was to wake her up. They both held still for a moment, waiting—but no sound came from the bedroom. They were safe. And in the quiet pause, Beth's anger had seeped away. She closed her book, then reached over and closed Adam's, too.

"Adam, listen to me. You have nothing to worry about."

"You don't know Kane . . ."

"Maybe I do, maybe I don't. But I know myself," she said urgently. "*You* know me. Whatever it is you think he's after, he's not going to get it."

Adam looked down and didn't respond.

"You trust me, right?"

"I do, of course I do, it's just that—"

"Look. Remember last month, when you were spending all that time with Kaia?" she asked.

A wary, panicked look flashed across Adam's face. "Yes . . ."

"And I was insanely jealous?"

"That's right, you were," he said triumphantly, vindicated.

"And you got mad, because I didn't trust you—and you were right."

He looked down again, deflated.

"I should have trusted you," Beth told him, "because I know you'd never do anything to hurt me."

"I never would," he said urgently. "Beth, you know that. I love you."

"And I love you." She leaned across the table and gave him a soft kiss on the lips. "And you just have to trust that. Okay?"

"So what now?" he asked.

She laughed. "Now you get out of here and let me get my work done so that I can see you another time. *Without* the stupid books."

He rolled his eyes. "Are you sure?" he asked, coming around to her side of the table and massaging her shoulders. As always, she melted beneath his warm and sure touch. "Because you might want to keep me around—I tend to come in handy."

She swatted him with her notebook. "Don't tempt me," she begged. "Now come on, get out."

He shrugged and turned to go. But he didn't get very far.

"Okay, come back," she cried. "You got me—one more kiss."

It was a long one.

Adam drove home. With the sweet taste of Beth still fresh on his lips—and the image of her in Kane's arms still fresh on his mind. He knew Kane—the guy got anything he wanted. Anything. Anyone. Adam had to work for everything he got; but for Kane, victory came easy. And it came often.

Beth could deny it all she wanted—she could beg him

to trust her a hundred times. But he couldn't help what he knew, and what he knew was that sometimes being in love, being trustworthy just isn't enough. Yes, he remembered back when he was spending all that time with Kaia. He'd sworn to Beth a million times that nothing would ever happen. And he'd meant it.

And it's not like he was some horrible person, he reminded himself. Kaia had just been there—the wrong girl, in the right place at the right time. He hadn't been able to stop himself. Sometimes he wasn't even sure he could blame himself—it had all seemed so inevitable. Sometimes, despite the best of intentions, things just happened.

And *that's* what he was afraid of.

chapter

8

That night, it seemed like sleep would never come.

Beth lay in bed, her body drained of energy, her mind spinning in circles, refusing to slow, refusing to relax. When had her life gotten so complicated? And what did it mean that the things that should have made her happy were the ones keeping her awake?

And, as long as she was asking meaningless questions that she'd never be able to answer, if she was so in love with her boyfriend, why did she sometimes wish he was someone else?

I wish I *were someone else,* she thought wistfully. Someone who didn't care so much about always doing the right thing and getting the job done, someone who wasn't overwhelmed by commitments and responsibilities to everyone in her life. *Someone who wasn't tied down to the same guy, day in and day out,* her mind whispered. To trade lives with someone, just for a day—was that so much to ask?

What would it be like, she wondered, to have Kaia's life? Not her striking beauty, or her wealth—though at the thought of a life free of skimping, saving, and scrounging, free of bussing tables at the diner and watching her parents drag themselves home from work at three a.m., Beth often felt a sharp pang of jealousy. There were people who lived life without struggling for every dollar. She'd accepted that she wasn't one of them—and while she didn't care as much as she used to, she cared. A lot. But looks, money, clothes, those were just things, possessions—Beth didn't want to *have* what Kaia *had*, she wanted, at least sometimes, secretly, late at night, to *be* who Kaia *was*. Beth often watched her out of the corner of her eye, marveling at the girl who seemed to float above the fray, skimming across the surface of life, never getting her feet dirty. It was such an alien frame of mind that Beth couldn't imagine how the world must seem to her. But on nights like this, she longed for it.

The apathetic manner, the almost inhuman poise—Kaia, she was sure, never fought with her boyfriends. Never questioned what she "really" wanted, and whether it was right or wrong. And, Beth was sure, never worried that her life was boring, that *she* was boring. Kaia was just like Kane in that way—and maybe, Beth suddenly realized, that was why she was so drawn to him, in spite of herself. And she was. Drawn to him. Even though she could only admit it to herself at times like this, alone, stranded between night and day, waiting for sleep—or sunrise.

It didn't matter, of course, because she was with Adam. Good, solid Adam. They were two peas in a pod. A perfect match. She knew that. She loved that. And yet . . .

He was the only boy she'd ever dated. The only boy

she'd ever held. Not that she was bored. She was just . . . curious. And if she could, for just one day, abandon herself, if she could leave good, dutiful Beth behind, if she could borrow Kaia's mind, Kaia's life—then she could know what it felt like to live without consequences, without guilt, to take whatever she wanted, to have it all. Just a one-day vacation from her cookie-cutter life, from always doing the right thing. That was all she asked.

Just one wild day.

And one wild night.

What had happened to her wild nights?

Sprawled across her Ralph Lauren sheets, her comforter kicked to the foot of the bed, Kaia opened her eyes with a sigh. She'd kept them closed as long as she could, hoping she could force sleep to come, but it wasn't working. She just wasn't tired—how could she be, when it was only one a.m. and she'd spent the night, like every night before it, lounging around her house?

Kaia's body was designed for a different life—she'd trained it well over the years, and by now it expected a steady influx of loud music, flashing lights, hot bodies, and cold drinks. Every night—all night. That had been her old life in her old world. She'd done her best to pretend that it had all disappeared when she left: the city, the social scene, her old friends. She preferred to think of it all as frozen in limbo, awaiting her return.

But when reality hit, it hit hard. The city was still bursting with life, her "friends" were still partying till dawn—and the only thing frozen in limbo was Kaia. She hated them for it, and she hated her parents for causing it. Most of all she hated the hours she spent every night, alone in the dark room, staring at the ceiling and wishing she could do something about the endless, deep quiet seeping into her bedroom from the desert outside. She could play music, turn up the volume on the TV, it didn't matter—somehow the desert silence managed to drown it all out. Made it impossible to forget how still everything was, and how empty—just like her life.

Most of the time Kaia clung to her memories of the past, to her hard-edged city persona, clung to it with a death grip, for fear of forgetting who she was and where she'd come from, fear of turning into a small-town zombie content with the simple life. But there were moments, fleeting but sharp, when she just wished she could let it all go. Everyone else in this stupid town was so happy, so satisfied—what must it be like, Kaia wondered, to be able to inhabit such a narrow world without feeling like the walls were closing in?

What must it be like to be Beth, too timid to complain about what you had, too dim to wonder if there might be something more? Kaia had been spending a lot of time recently watching Beth, wondering how her mind might work—and sometimes, to her horror, she'd actually wished she could, just for a moment, switch places with the girl. She had such a picture-perfect life—loving parents, loving boyfriend—all the things Kaia had never wanted, never thought she needed. And it was true, she didn't *need* someone lying beside her, holding her, whispering that he loved her and that everything would be okay. She didn't *need* to know if her mother missed her, or if her father would ever stop home for more than a night. That kind of thing was no more than a security blanket for the Beths of the world. It was just that late at night, alone and empty, Kaia sometimes wished she were one of them.

Beth, she was sure, didn't stay up nights desperate for excitement, searching for trouble. Beth wasn't constantly bored, restless, always on the hunt for the next hot spot, the next hot guy. Beth didn't spend every minute wishing she were somewhere else, doing something else. Being someone else. No, when your life was placid, when you had what you wanted, no more and no less, you slept like a baby. It was only when you were dissatisfied, when your life seemed empty and you had nothing to fill it with, that you tossed and turned. Until finally, as always, you gave up on sleep and turned on the light.

Adam awoke with a start and flicked on the light, gasping with the relief of escaping a nightmare. He didn't remember much of it, only that it had featured Beth and Kaia—and it had left him drenched in a cold sweat. He sat up in bed and took a few deep breaths, trying to wash all traces of the nightmare out of his mind so that he could safely fall back asleep.

His sleep had been filled with nightmares for weeks. They'd started the night after he slept with Kaia, and ever since Kane and Beth had started spending all that time together, his dreams had only gotten worse. Too much stress, he told himself, lying back down on the mattress. Adam had always liked to keep things simple. But now? Nothing was simple, not anymore. Certainly not his relationship with Beth. That was a minefield. When he was with her, he struggled over his every word, agonized over every action, searching fruitlessly for the magic combination that would put right whatever had gone wrong.

Nothing worked. And lately it seemed like everything that came out of his mouth just made things worse.

Kane, on the other hand, always knew the right thing to say. Adam could see it in Beth's eyes—"Why can't you be more like him?" She would never say it out loud, but he knew her well enough to read her thoughts, to know her desires. Kane was flashy, charismatic, Kane saw what he wanted and took it—and girls loved that. Adam had always thought Beth was different. But now . . . he wasn't so sure.

Just once, he thought in frustration, *just once, I'd like to know what it's like.* To win, every time, without trying. To effortlessly be the best, and have the world at your fingertips. Everything Adam had, he had only because Kane hadn't thought it worth the trouble. Kane got good grades without studying, beat Adam on the courts without breaking a sweat, could get any girl he wanted just by curling up a corner of his lip in that famous Kane smirk. Adam worked so hard, at everything—and yet time and time again, it seemed he was always coming in second.

But Beth hadn't been seduced by the flash or the glitter of Kane's charm—Beth had chosen Adam. She'd been repulsed by Kane, she always told him, and seduced by Adam's straightforward manner, his honest appeal. It had been the first time he and Kane had ever gone head-to-head over a girl—and the first competition Adam had ever truly won. But it seemed the battle had never really ended. And maybe he hadn't won after all.

Adam had never wanted to be Kane, had never even much admired Kane. But if only he could just borrow a little of whatever it was that allowed him to lead a charmed life. Adam was sure that Kane would never have gotten sucked in by Kaia's act, would never have been fooled into believing anything she said. Kane would know exactly the right thing to say to get his girlfriend past the whole virgin issue—and he'd do it so smoothly that she would think it had been her idea. And Kane would never, *never* let another guy sweep his girlfriend off her feet. Kane didn't get brushed aside, ignored, overlooked. Ever.

Kane had "it," whatever it was. And Adam just didn't. Instead, he had a work ethic, a conscience, and a face that couldn't lie. And, for now, he had Beth.

But with Kane on the prowl, how long would that last?

How long could it last, this merry sidekick game, before she got fed up? Miranda lay flat on her back in bed, her eyes tracing the tiny cracks in the white ceiling paint. She'd stayed up late, shampooing and shampooing until finally she'd managed to wash most of the green out of her hair. She hoped.

And now she'd been lying in bed for the past hour, trying to work up some kind of excitement about this dunk tank guy, trying to picture his body curled up against her in the bed, his hands crawling across her body . . . but it wasn't working. She kept losing her concentration, and his face kept morphing into Kane's. She didn't have to *work* at desiring Kane—it was the easiest thing she'd ever done. Imagining herself in Kane's arms seemed as natural as breathing. Maybe because she had so much practice.

She knew what Harper had said—and she knew Harper was right—but still, did she have to like it? She didn't see Harper forcing herself to date a loser, just because her first choice was "temporarily" unavailable.

But of course, that was Harper. Miranda sighed. You'd think she would be used to this by now. She'd been playing second fiddle to Harper since elementary school. "Partners in crime," that's what they always called themselves—but when she was alone, Miranda sometimes wondered. It didn't feel like a partnership. It felt like Harper was out for herself, leaving Miranda to follow behind, cleaning up her messes.

Miranda shook away such disloyal thoughts. Just because Harper could be a little thoughtless, a little self-centered at times, was no reason to question her commitment. Maybe there was only one problem in this friendship: Just maybe, Miranda was jealous. She would never have admitted it out loud, but there were times—*lots* of times—when she looked at Harper and asked herself, *Why not me?* They'd started in the same place as wild, spunky outcasts, gone through all the same experiences—and yet Harper had blossomed into this alpha queen, while Miranda, it sometimes seemed, had never blossomed at all.

What did Harper have that she didn't?

Beauty, she reminded herself.

Charisma.

Sex appeal.

And confidence.

Maybe that's all it was—Harper knew what she wanted, and she believed she deserved it. So she went out and did whatever it took. Miranda, on the other hand? She knew what she wanted, beat herself up about it, then sat on her hands and did nothing.

And, when it came to Kane, it seemed Harper agreed with her—she wasn't worthy. Didn't deserve the guy of her dreams, apparently. She deserved to settle for something attainable, something subpar.

Miranda was no hanger-on, clinging to a friendship with Harper in the hopes that some small crumbs of desirability and popularity would fall to the ground at her feet. But a part of her was always waiting, wondering—when would Harper turn to her and say, "It's your turn now"? When would she reveal her secret of success and teach Miranda how to be bold, beautiful, and . . . more like Harper?

After all, everyone knew Harper Grace had it all—so wasn't there enough to share?

Harper had never been very good at the sharing thing. Maybe it came from being an only child. Or maybe it just came from her utter disdain for almost everyone who crossed her path. Why should she share? Who was more deserving than her of having . . . well, anything?

Which isn't to say that there weren't a few exceptions— obviously there were some people worth her time and goodwill. Well, at least two: Miranda and Adam.

But then, she wasn't very good at sharing them, either. Which is why she'd hated Beth even before discovering her own feelings for Adam. Harper was supposed to be his top priority, and always had been. But when Beth showed up, everything changed. She'd stomped all over Harper and Adam's friendship, pulled him away; even if she hadn't been in love, Harper doubted she would have been able to stand it for very long.

She wouldn't have to wait much longer, Harper comforted herself. The next day, she was planning to put Kaia's plan into action. There was just one thing: What if it didn't work?

Harper rolled over in bed, kicking at her blankets in frustration. She hated thinking of Beth, wanting what Beth had—*Beth*, of all people. So boring, so dull—she was nothing, compared to Harper. And yet she had the one thing that Harper wanted the most.

And it wasn't just Beth. Kaia'd had him too.

It was infuriating, the way Harper couldn't stop watching her enemies—even her friends—and wishing she had what they had. She would never want Beth's life, Beth's bland and muddled personality. So why did she spend so much time wishing she could take Beth's place?

It was the same with Kaia, spoiled, self-centered, bitchy, *rich* Kaia. She had no friends, no life—but she had so much else. Harper looked around at her room with complete disgust. The shoddy pieces of furniture, shadowy silhouettes in the moonlight, were supposedly antiques, but to her they just seemed old and out of style. Her closet was bursting with imitation designer gear, discount shoes—and even those, her parents always claimed, were practically more than they could afford. Whereas Kaia was probably spread out on designer sheets beneath a mahogany four-poster bed, tucked away in a cozy corner of her giant estate. Kaia didn't have to buy Frada (imitation Prada), and she didn't have to worry that someone from school would spot her helping out at the family dry cleaning store on weekends.

Sometimes it seemed like everyone she knew had something she wanted. Money, men—it didn't end there.

She was even jealous of Adam's good-natured honesty, Kane's car—and his complete lack of scruples. Even Miranda had something Harper occasionally longed for: obscurity. She didn't have to worry about people watching, judging her every move. She didn't have to constantly perform. She could just *be*.

It was as if everyone had *something*, something that made their lives better, special—and what did Harper have?

For one thing, she had the admiration of every kid in school. But, late at night, deep in the back of her mind, a small voice questioned what they saw when they looked at her. Was it real? Or did it all rest on an elaborate bluff?

Because if Harper really was who they said she was, if she really did have anything a girl could ever want, why did she lie awake so many nights wishing she were someone— almost *anyone*—else?

Anyone else might have lain awake all night, every night, struggling with his conscience, worrying about his betrayal of a friend, wondering if he was doing the right thing.

Not Kane.

No, as he stretched himself out along the couch and tucked a thin blanket over himself, his mind was untroubled, his conscience clear.

And he did have a conscience—despite his constant boasts to the contrary. True, it didn't get much of a work-out. But it was, like everything else about Kane, fully functioning—and, he insisted to himself, in this case it just had nothing to say.

He flicked on the TV—he needed it to fall asleep, to fill the silence of his empty house—and closed his eyes.

So he was in hot pursuit of Adam's girlfriend. So what? First, as he'd pointed out to Harper, he and Adam weren't best friends. Spending time with people didn't automatically make you close, it didn't mean you could depend on them. He'd learned that the hard way, a long time ago. And he wasn't about to make the same mistake again. He liked Adam, liked hanging out with him—he certainly outclassed the rest of the Haven High gang of losers—but they didn't owe each other anything.

Second, Beth was just a girl. Sure, Adam would be broken up, for a while—but he'd recover.

And then, there was the third issue. The status of his so-called crime: Was it even possible to steal something that had already been stolen? Because Kane had spotted Beth first. Kane had pursued Beth first. And by the rules of the game—rules that, in the old days, Adam had readily agreed to—Beth had been his for the taking. Until Adam swooped in and took her away. Beth had forgotten. Adam had forgotten.

But Kane remembered.

She had chosen Adam over Kane. She'd fallen for Adam's good-boy looks, his good-boy charm. She'd brushed Kane away from her like a gnat and given herself to Adam. And ever since then, everything had been different. Adam was different, ignoring every other girl, most of the time ignoring Kane—all he wanted was Beth. To be with her, to talk about her, to hold her. Kane couldn't stand it. Partly because he hated to see a friend morph into one of those relationship pod people, jettisoning all the interesting parts of his personality. Trying his best to behave—to obey.

But more than that, Kane couldn't stand the possibility that Beth wasn't "just a girl," that she really was something special, something new—and that she belonged to someone else. Kane was not, by nature, a covetous person. Envy was too passive for him. To envy something, after all, you had to be sitting on the sidelines, watching what someone else had. Wanting it, longing for it, and powerless to get it.

Kane didn't do powerless. He didn't waste his time wishing he had someone else's life, someone else's possessions. He was who he was, he had what he had—and when he discovered something out there in the world that he needed? He took it.

chapter

9

Harper didn't usually associate with Beth and her little clique during gym class. Of course she had to be nice to Adam's girlfriend, and *pretend* they were friends, but that didn't mean they needed to be bosom buddies. So usually, after suffering through the forty-five minutes of torture better known as phys ed, she stayed on the other side of the locker room, sliding out of her hideous orange and black uniform and back into her real clothes as quickly as possible so that she could get the hell out. (The girls' locker room, although lacking the overpowering stench of sweat ever-present in the guys' locker room, was still not the type of place in which you wanted to kick back and relax.) But today was different. Today she had a mission. Kane and Harper had conferred, and agreed: It was time to set Kaia's plan into motion.

She moved into position—a few feet away from Beth and the group of mousy blondes who surrounded her.

When Beth, with her watered-down personality, managed to be the center of attention, you had to wonder about the quality of the company. Imagine a group that found the Queen of Bland riveting, Harper marveled to herself.

Far enough away to be unobtrusive, but close enough to . . . to do what she had to do.

She felt a small twinge of guilt about the whole thing, but quickly squelched it. She was doing all of them a favor, she reminded herself. Beth and Adam's rickety relationship was being held together by a Band-Aid—and it would be less painful for all involved if someone just ripped it off, nice and quick.

Lucky for them all, Harper was up to the task.

"God, if I never have to run laps again, it'll be way too soon," Marcy sighed, stripping out of her sweaty gym uniform.

"Who invented gym, anyway?" Marcy's best friend, Darcy, chimed in.

Beth laughed, letting the familiar chatter wash over her. It was the same every week with these girls: Gym sucked. School sucked. Guys rocked. Gym sucked. Rinse and repeat.

They weren't her friends, exactly—beyond Marcy and Darcy (one never went anywhere without the other), they weren't even friends with one another. But they were all dating guys on the team—the swim team, the basketball team, the lacrosse team, depending on the season. It didn't really matter. At a school this small, there was pretty much only one Team. And whatever the season, Adam was its captain. Which somehow made Beth—what, exactly? She was never sure. Not the most popular, certainly. That would always be Harper, who kept herself aloof from "the girl-friends" but still managed to gain their unadulterated admiration. Not the best liked—for Beth was unsure whether these girls actually *liked* anyone. She was certain, however, that if she and Adam ever broke up, the flock of giggling girls would disappear along with him. But at the moment she seemed to have a certain cachet. It was as if they were all drawn to one another by some elusive girl-friend pheromone, and hers was—by virtue of dating Adam, Big Man on Campus—the strongest. Maybe it was some kind of evolutionary reflex.

Or maybe you've just been spending too much time staring at your AP bio book, she thought, laughing at herself and her insatiable need to overanalyze everything. Why couldn't she just accept these girls for whatever they were? Comfortable acquaintances, just another perk of dating Adam, like free tickets to football games and a ride to school whenever she needed one.

So what if they were vain and vapid? It's not like she could afford to be choosy—she didn't have too many friends these days, beyond Adam. So she should probably stop being so judgmental and just take what she could get.

"So *are* you, Beth?" Marcy asked insistently.

"Am I what?" Beth asked in confusion, suddenly real-izing all eyes were on her. She pulled off her gym uniform and began brushing out her long, blond hair. Back in ninth grade, when she'd walked into the locker room for the first time, she'd been insanely bashful about letting the other girls see her change. Over the course of a few months, she even developed a system of contortions that would allow her to change from her clothes into her gym uniform and back again without revealing a square of naked flesh to anyone. Four years later the whole thing seemed ridiculous. She was totally comfortable now wandering around the locker room in her underwear—it was just another part of the high school experience, like cafeteria food. And trigonometry. She couldn't even remember what her problem had been. Of course, she mused, back then *no one* ever saw her naked, and the very thought of revealing herself to another person had made her skin crawl. Then came Adam.

"Are you going to the championships?" Darcy repeated on behalf of her best friend. "You heard the student council got together enough funds to pay for a bus to take us all up to Valley Glen, right?"

"Yeah, I heard." Beth smiled, remembering how delighted Adam had been when she told him she would finally be there to see him swim. And hopefully, win. This year's regionals were being held at Valley Glen High, a huge school up north, and a school bus had been chartered to take half of Haven High along to cheer on the swimmers. (Given the football team's 0–9 record—three years in a row—Haven fans had plenty of time and energy on their hands.) It would be a long day, but Beth wouldn't miss it for anything. She knew how important it was to Adam. And seeing how much he wanted her there had just reminded her how much he loved her. And how much she loved him. Not that spending five hours on a bus with Marcy, Darcy, and the rest of the Haven High cheering section sounded particularly appealing to her—but it would be worth it to get to see Adam in action again, to show him that she cared. Besides, she'd promised him. She was, after all, his good luck charm. "I'm definitely going," she answered, grinning. "I can hardly wait."

"Looks like you won't have to," Marcy said.

"What do you mean?"

"Weren't you listening?" Darcy asked. "We were just talking about how great it is that they rescheduled the championships for this week."

"This week?" Beth asked in alarm. "But the SATs are on Saturday!"

"Exactly, that's what's so great—you know they're giving the seniors Thursday and Friday off."

"So we can *study*," Beth pointed out.

Darcy laughed. "Yeah, but who's actually going to do that? No, it's perfect—we'll ride up on Thursday morning, watch the meet, do some victory partying, and then ride back late that night. And we have all of Friday to sleep it off!"

"Are you sure about this?" Beth asked, her throat tightening.

"Yeah, Kyle just told me."

Kyle was Darcy's boyfriend, and the swim team's cocaptain. If he'd said it, it must be true.

Shit.

"I can't do that, I can't go away two days before the test," she cried. "That's insane."

"Breathe, Beth. It's no big deal. It's just . . ."

But Beth tuned out the rest of the prattle, her mind frantically racing to find a way around the problem. There wasn't one. She was just going in circles, always coming back to the same basic certainty.

She was going to have to back out—and Adam was going to freak.

As the rest of the girls filtered out of the locker room, Harper lingered. Once she was on her own, she snapped open her cell and quickly flipped through the images she'd captured. Perfect. She'd gotten everything she needed— and more. This swim meet development was quite the windfall.

That had been the only flaw in Kaia's ruthlessly brilliant plan—the when. And now Beth had supplied them with the perfect solution. If Adam went out to Valley Glen and Beth stayed here . . . Well, if she'd had any doubts before about whether this was the right thing to do, they were gone now. Why else would all this good luck be raining down on her if this weren't exactly what she was meant to do? Why else was everything working out even better than expected?

It would be the ideal setup, but it would mean they had to move fast. And Kane, who was on the swim team too (at least when he felt like going to practice) would have to give up a shot at athletic glory—somehow, Harper was pretty sure he wouldn't care. Why would he want to go all the way to Valley Glen for a pathetic plastic trophy, when the real trophy would be right here, conveniently close to home?

She slipped out of the locker room and sprinted down the hall to e-mail Kane and Kaia. They needed to know that step one was taken care of and step two needed to happen ASAP. Beth had just dumped a giant gift in their laps. It would be a shame to let it go to waste.

✧✧✧

Beth steeled herself all day for the inevitable. But when the moment came, she still wasn't ready. She sat in the car next to him, looking out the window as the familiar scenery whizzed by, nodding absently as he filled her in on the details of his day at school. She was too nervous to pay much attention, instead plotting out the conversation in her mind, striving for some angle that wouldn't cause an eruption. She'd yet to find one—but a couple miles from her house, she realized she just couldn't wait any longer.

"I've got bad news," she blurted out, interrupting some story about his history teacher's toupee.

He flicked his eyes off the road for a quick second, flashing her a look of concern. "What is it?"

"It's your swimming championships."

"Oh, right, I've been meaning to tell you, there was some kind of scheduling screw-up, so they changed the date and—"

"I can't go," she said flatly.

"What?"

Something suddenly occurred to her—and she didn't like it. "Adam, if you knew they'd changed the date, why didn't you tell me?" she asked suspiciously.

"I was about to," he said uncomfortably.

"It's two days before the SATs—you *knew* I wouldn't be able to do that."

"Yeah—wouldn't *want* to do that."

"Wouldn't want to blow the test, no," she agreed. He could be such a baby sometimes. "Look, I'll come see you some other time, I promise."

"Some other time? This is *it*, Beth, this is the time. It's the end of the season—it's the championships, for God's sake. I thought you understood that this was important to me."

"And the SATs are important to *me*," she retorted. "Look, it's not like I'm asking you not to go."

"No, you're just saying you can't be bothered to come along," he countered.

"Don't do that." She was getting so sick of having the same conversation again and again. Was she supposed to plan her entire life around him? "Don't try to make this about you and me. You know this test means everything to me."

"And I don't?"

She was running out of patience—if she wanted to spend the afternoon dealing with a whiny child, she'd be home babysitting her little brothers.

"Adam, it's not that I don't want to be there for you— but this is my life we're talking about here. I can't throw everything away for some stupid swim meet."

"Right," he muttered. "When it's something you care about, it's important. When it's something I care about, it's just stupid."

Beth sighed. "That's not what I meant, and you know it. I wish I could go, Adam, I do," she said desperately. "I just *can't*—I mean, if it were some other weekend. *Any* other weekend. This just isn't the time."

He gripped the wheel tightly. "It's *never* the time. You just don't get it, do you? You and me, we need—I need— can't you just *make* the time?"

"*You* just don't get it," Beth cried, as all the anger and frustration she'd been suppressing for the past few weeks bubbled to the surface and burst through. "Why do you have to be like this? Why can't you understand that this is my future we're talking about? It's your future too," she pointed out, even though she'd promised herself she would never bring this up, wouldn't try to force him to see what he was missing out on. "It wouldn't hurt you to do a little studying of your own. I mean, even Kane—"

She cut herself off, realizing as soon as his name came out of her mouth that she'd made a serious mistake. But it was too late.

"So that's what this is about?" Adam snarled. "I knew it."

"No, that has nothing to do with what this is about. Why can't you just let this go?"

"Are you seeing him tonight?" he asked in a low, calm voice.

"Yes, but—"

"And tomorrow?"

"Adam—"

"And I guess *he'll* be ditching the swim team, staying here with you for some hot and heavy studying while your boyfriend conveniently goes out of town?"

"You got me!" she cried. "You figured out my secret plan. As soon as you get out of town, Kane and I are just going to hop into bed together. That's all you care about, isn't it? Not spending time with me—keeping me away from him!"

Adam stared straight ahead at the road, fingers tightly clenching the wheel. The car suddenly felt very, very small. "I didn't realize that staying away from him would be such a sacrifice."

"I'm not your property, Adam. You don't get to tell me who to spend time with. And acting like this isn't the best way to keep me from cheating on you—or breaking up with you."

"What is the best way, then? You tell me. Because I'm beginning to think there isn't one. You're just going to do whatever you want to, no matter what I say."

"You're right," Beth spluttered, barely able to believe the words that were coming out of her mouth. She would *never* cheat on Adam—and she'd never throw away her relationship just to preserve some barely-there friendship with Kane. But that was *her* decision to make. Not his. "If you want someone who's just going to take orders from you, follow you around like you're her almighty ruler, you're dating the wrong girl."

"Maybe I am," he agreed angrily.

"You know what? Stop the car."

"What?"

"Stop the car. I'm getting out. I can't be around you when you're like this."

He glanced over at her incredulously. "You want me to stop the car and let you out on an empty road in the middle of nowhere?"

"Anything would be better than being stuck in this car with you," she said, her voice filled with spite.

"Fine." He swerved to the side of the road, slammed on the brakes, and the car skidded to a stop. "Get out. See if I care what happens to you."

"Oh, don't worry, I know you don't. You've made that painfully clear."

"Don't try to—"

But she slammed the door in his face, and his voice trailed off as he saw she was serious. She turned away from the car and began walking slowly down the narrow shoulder of the road. At that rate, it would take her an hour to get home from there—and it was getting dark.

Adam knew he should pull up alongside her and try to persuade her to get back into the car. If that failed, he should drive beside her the whole way home, just to make sure nothing happened.

It was the right thing to do. He knew that.

And he really meant to do it, right up until the moment he put the car in gear and pressed a leaden foot down on the gas pedal. The tires screeched as the car peeled onto the road and sped past her solitary figure.

By the time he'd calmed down enough to realize what he'd done, she had long since disappeared into the dark distance. He could have turned around. Gone back for her.

But he didn't.

Kaia's favorite French film was part of a trilogy: *Bleu*, *Blanc*, and *Rouge*. She'd seen all three in a row during a foreign film festival at Lincoln Center. One rainy day, she'd barricaded herself in the theater and, shivering in her Anna Sui raincoat, she'd fallen in love. The best of the three, she'd decided, was *Bleu*. The plot was elegant and obscure: A young, beautiful woman loses everything, everything that matters. She is alone, disconnected, disenchanted, and free. Ultimate freedom, at the ultimate price. Death of the spirit—and, ultimately, a reawakening.

It was intense, it was sexy, and it was the way Kaia

wanted her world to be. Elegant, beautiful people, awash in a cool, bluish gray light, speaking in clipped sentences packed with suppressed passion and cryptic meaning.

So it was this DVD that she tucked into a picnic basket, along with some gourmet cheese imported directly from a small farm in the French Alps, and a bottle of Bordeaux snagged from her father's ample wine cellar, before setting off for Jack Powell's house. It was time for Little Red Riding Hood to pay a call on the Big Bad Wolf.

She wasn't completely sure that now was the time to make her final move—though it was quite obvious the move would need to be hers. He wasn't about to take the step. But was he ready yet? Oh, she saw the glint in his eyes when he looked at her, the hint of desire in his voice every time he told her to go away. And the spark between them when they'd touched the other night, that couldn't be denied.

Yes, she told herself once again. *He's ready.*

And so was she.

She wore a filmy black slip dress and strappy black kitten heels. And beneath it all, a custom-made camisole of red lace, and black panties with a red lace trim. She looked good, *all over.* And she knew it.

She rang the doorbell, savoring the nervous energy fizzing inside of her—it was rare, these days, that a guy could set her blood boiling with anticipation, that the thrill of the chase came paired with the arousing fear of rejection. It was one of the reasons she wanted this so badly. That, and the way his designer shirts hung on his sculpted body, the sound of his elegant British accent, his easy charm, his icy anger.

He was the complete package. And it was such a turn-on.

He opened the door, unlike her dressed down for the night—adorably rumpled hair, tight jeans, Oxford T-shirt. His eyes widened when he saw what was waiting on his front doorstep.

"You," he said simply, blocking the entranceway to the house.

"Me." She smiled.

"You're out kind of late," he finally observed. "Won't Mommy and Daddy be wondering where their precious little one has run off to?"

"Daddy's off screwing his secretary in a Vegas hotel room, and Mommy's back in Manhattan, probably having a nice, long sleep courtesy of Dr. Valium," she informed him bitterly. "So . . . no."

"What's in the basket?"

She pulled out the wine. "Reinforcements."

He looked down the dark and deserted street.

"Did anyone see you? Does anyone know you're here?"

"What do you think?"

"I think you're trouble," he reminded her. "But as I recall, we've already had that conversation."

"Ad nauseam . . . are we ready for a new one?"

He looked her up and down, then sighed appreciatively. "You are *not* what I expected when I came out to this hick town."

"Ditto. So—what do you want to do about it?"

There was a pause, and a palpable tension in the air. This was the moment, she knew. He was on the brink, and it was now that he would either step back to safety—or grab her wrist and plunge them both into the depths.

He took a deep breath. "There are going to be some rules."

"Of course." She nodded, disguising her relief. Now they were getting somewhere.

"No one can know."

She rolled her eyes.

"*No one,*" he repeated.

"Yes, sir." She saluted.

"No other guys."

"I don't see how that's any of your—"

"High school boys get jealous," he explained. "When they get jealous, they get curious. And *that* I don't need."

"Right. No extracurricular activities," she agreed. She had the sneaking suspicion this wasn't the first time he'd had this conversation. He was too quick, too smooth.

"And no more of this stalking nonsense. I don't want you showing up in my classroom, in my bar, at my house— we meet *when* I say, *where* I say. I don't like surprises."

Kaia gave him a slow, simmering smile.

"Then you're going to hate me."

His face remained frozen. "Are we agreed?"

"Completely."

"You break the rules, and we end this," he warned her. "Immediately. I'm not some horny teenager who's so desperate to get some that I'm willing to throw my life away."

Could have fooled me, Kaia thought, wondering—not for the first time—what had brought a man like that to a town like this.

But if he wanted to believe he was in control, that was just fine with her.

"Your wish is my command, *Jack*."

"In that case, what are you waiting for?"

She took a step toward him, tilting her head up as if to seal the deal with a kiss, but he backed away and shook his head.

"Not out here," he chided her. "Never where people can see." He swung the door open a bit wider and stepped aside, ushering her in with an exaggerated sweep of his arm.

No matter, she could wait. For another minute or two, at least. And then, she thought, pausing in the doorway and marveling at his cocky good looks and the sizzling current of sexual tension flowing between them—then all bets were off.

She stepped inside the house, and Powell slammed the door shut behind her.

Waiting time was over.

chapter

10

The next day they met at dusk.

When Kane pulled up in his silver Camaro, Adam was already on the court. He'd arrived a half hour before and had spent the time running up and down the length of the court, slamming the ball into the cool concrete, sinking shot after shot. Warming up. Practicing. Kane, he knew, had called him out here for a friendly game of ball. Nice and easy. That was the thing, wasn't it?

Adam slammed the ball against the backboard. Nice and easy. Story of Kane's life. You want something? You take it. Just like that. Kane, who got good grades without studying. Who had every girl chasing after him despite being an unapologetically sexist pig. Who was the best basketball player in town despite the fact that he was too lazy to practice, too above it all to join the team.

He won everything, always—every game, every argument, every girl.

And all without even trying.

Adam slammed the ball again, harder.

Not this time. Everyone had to lose sometime. Everyone.

The game started off slow. Friendly. Nice and easy. But then Kane scored. And scored again.

And Adam began to simmer. And the angrier he got, the harder he tried, the harder he gripped the ball, the harder he threw it. What should have been a smoothly arced two-pointer became a spasmodic air ball; what should have been an easy layup bounced off the rim. And every time, Kane grabbed the rebound.

He shot.

He scored.

"Dude, what's up with you today? You're playing like a girl," Kane taunted him.

Adam ran past his opponent, giving him a hard shove with his left shoulder and grabbing the ball as Kane fell backward.

He shot and, finally, scored.

And it felt good.

"And your problem is . . . ?" Kane asked, picking himself up off the ground.

"No problem," Adam replied, suddenly whipping the ball toward Kane, whose lightening fast reflexes caught it just before it smashed into his nose.

"Hey, watch the face—I'm nothing if I'm not pretty."

"Tell me about it," Adam growled.

"Oh, I get it," Kane said, dribbling down the court with swift, sure movements.

"Get what?" Adam asked irritably.

He lunged for the ball, but Kane veered away, faking left, then cutting right as Adam's hands swiped uselessly at the empty air.

"You're tired of always coming in second," Kane said, tossing in another basket. "You're always the runner-up, I'm always the champ. You're tired of being a loser."

It was nothing more than their standard trash talk. They always did it. You got a rise out of your opponent, put him off his game. Kane, to be sure, had made a science of it—and used the same technique off the court to keep his opponents equally off balance. Today shouldn't have been different from any other day, but it was. Today Adam just wasn't in the mood.

"Shut up," he snapped, grabbing the ball away and dribbling it down the court. Kane hounded him, but Adam knocked him off balance again, this time with a sharp jab in the stomach.

Kane dropped to the ground with a soft sigh, as if all the air had been let out of him, and Adam raced for the basket with a spurt of renewed, righteous energy. His path was clear, his mind was clear, and the basket lay straight ahead.

He got into position, readied the ball on his fingertips, imagining its perfect three-point arc ending in a nearly silent *swoosh*.

"By the way," Kane said nonchalantly, still on the ground where Adam had left him. "If I see your girlfriend tonight, should I tell her you say hello?"

Air ball.

After the basketball game ended—rather abruptly—Kane rushed home to shower and change, then drove right back to school. He met Kaia and Harper in front of the dark building, their figures illuminated by the low-watt yellowish lights. Kane pulled out his key—he had keys for almost every door in town—and they slipped inside.

There was always something about being in the school after hours, after dark. An illicit thrill, the undercurrent of tension and excitement—the possibility of getting caught. The halls that were so familiar and oppressive during the day transformed into a dark, shadowy no-man's-land for them to explore.

It made no sense—sneaking *into* school would likely get them into no more trouble than sneaking out of it, which all three of them did on a regular basis. But there was still something there—an unspoken feeling that just by being there at this hour, alone in the dark, they had somehow taken ownership of a side of the school its true owners had never known.

Of course, in a sense, they owned the school during the daylight hours too—so it wasn't a big leap of the imagination.

They crept down the hallway, single file, keeping an eye out for the janitor. Kane went first, leading the way, unable to stop dwelling on the game. It had been so easy to get a rise out of Adam—it was the kind of thing he did best. A skill that had always made him proud. At least in the past.

Next came Kaia, silently marveling at the excitement and nervous energy churning in her stomach, despite the fact that this little caper was far tamer than many she'd successfully pulled off on the East Coast. Maybe it had something to do with the night before—the touch of Jack Powell's body had lit up something inside of her, something that had lain dormant for a long time.

And finally, Harper. Decked out in trespassing haute couture (black faux cashmere sweater, dark jeans, Sketchers sneakers in place of her usual heels, the better for softly padding through the empty halls). She gripped the bag holding Kane's digital camera tightly. Things were going so smoothly, so perfectly—was something about to happen to screw everything up? Or should she just accept that the universe was on her side, guiding her toward an inescapable destiny?

Kane led them to the girls' locker room, unlocked the door, and flicked on the lights. They squinted in the sudden brightness, then got down to business. Harper pointed out Beth's locker—it probably wouldn't matter much on the small screen, but they'd agreed that the backgrounds should match as exactly as possible.

Then Kaia took the camera and Harper stripped off her shirt—her height and body type were closest to Beth's, and again, they'd agreed this was best. She unbuttoned her jeans, but then paused.

"Bashful, Grace?" Kane asked, chuckling. His laugh echoed through the room, bouncing off the grubby linoleum and washing over them. He'd already stripped down to his silk boxers. "Come on, it's nothing I haven't seen before."

She sneered at him. Stripping down in front of Kane was no big deal—it was the camera she couldn't stop thinking about. And not just because, when it came to kinky fun, she'd never been into the whole Kodak moment scene. It was more that seeing the camera made it real. What they were about to do—and who it was going to hurt. Harper knew she could put a stop to the whole thing in a second—just call it off, send everyone home.

Instead, she peeled off her jeans.

"You do know how to sweet talk a girl," she said sarcastically. "I know we all look the same to you."

"Well . . . that may be true," Kane admitted. "But in this case, I mean *you're* nothing I haven't seen before. Or are we forgetting that fateful day after Shayna's eighth-grade birthday blowout?"

"Kane," Harper said warningly, shooting a glance at Kaia, whose affected veneer of boredom couldn't disguise her sudden interest. Harper and Kane had vowed never to speak of The Incident again. And never had—until now.

"I, for one, remember it *very* well," Kane mused. "You, me, a jug of grain alcohol. Good times, good times."

"Kane! Shut up." She balled up her jeans and threw them at him. He caught the denim missile easily and tossed it back to her.

"Chill out, I'm just trying to lighten things up. Just reminding you that my arms are not such an alien place for you to be."

Harper rolled her eyes. "I'll never understand how you manage to get anyone to fall for that dirtbag 'charm' of yours," she complained.

"Ask Beth—she's falling for it, hook, line, and sinker."

At that, Kaia cleared her throat and waved the camera in the air.

"Guys? Speaking of Beth, maybe we should get a move on with the task at hand? Much as I'm enjoying the Harper and Kane show, I don't really need to spend the rest of the night watching you two practice flirtatious banter."

Kane nodded. "You're right, enough flirting—"

"*That* was flirting?" Harper interjected. "We really are in trouble."

"Like I was saying," Kane continued, staring down

Harper, "enough flirting, down to business." He mugged for Kaia and the camera. "Come on, I'm ready for my close up, Ms. DeMille."

"Okay then, hotshot, let's get started. Nice and slow."

The next hour passed in a blur, a steamy montage of sexy poses and ever-changing camera angles.

Here was Harper draped in Kane's arms, her head resting on his bare chest.

Flash, click.

And Kane tracing his fingers down Harper's bare back.

Click.

Harper and Kane pressed together, their lips locked in a kiss.

Click.

And more, and more, and more.

Not that Harper was enjoying the rubbing and the pressing and the groping and the kissing of the fake hookup. And not that Kane was turned on by the warm, supple body writhing in his arms, her mind committed to someone else, her body all his. Kaia, certainly, could not have been taking a secret thrill from the voyeurism of it all, playing the puppet master, barking out commands, suggesting poses, capturing it all on film.

All three of them, they assured themselves, would never sink low enough to actually enjoy the depravity.

Still, when the pictures were all taken, the arms and legs untangled, the clothes back on, all three were sorry to see the evening end.

"Well, it's been fun, ladies," Kane said, grabbing the camera and flipping appreciatively through the stills they'd captured. "You look *good*, Grace."

"You're not going to start chasing after *me* now, are you?" Harper asked, feigning disgust.

"Oh, don't be so full of yourself. You may look good," he pointed out, "but I look better."

"On that note, should we get out of here?" Kaia suggested. "I think we got what we needed."

"Here's my cell, Kane." Harper handed over her phone, with its own stock of photos still intact. "So you're sure you can actually make this work?"

"Have no fear—my Photoshop skills are second only to my carnal skills—and you've got personal confirmation of those."

"Gross, don't remind me," Harper complained, smacking his chest good-naturedly. "Come on, let's go—I think after that, we could all use a drink."

They crept out as silently as they'd crept in, and drove off together into the dark night, the cell phone and digital camera safe and sound in Kane's bag. It was the dynamite that would blow Beth and Adam's relationship apart—and the fuse had just been lit.

The dunk tank guy, Greg, had been only too eager to take Miranda for dinner, and they'd met at seven that night at the one nice restaurant in town. It turned out he was a junior (a bit embarrassing, but not nearly as bad as if he'd been a sophomore), and when he wasn't dressed like a cowboy, he was at least passably cute. Or at least acceptable. The ears were still too big and the thick-framed glasses still a no go, but she could at least handle the freckles. After all, they matched her own.

The dinner itself had gone, well . . . okay. Miranda was

wearing the sexy new outfit she'd impulse bought the other day, and while she was still slightly afraid it made her look like a thick-trunked tree, she told herself she probably looked okay. And Greg, once you stripped away the nervousness that apparently made him act like a dick, was a pretty nice guy with an easy laugh. He seemed fun, witty, smart, and—what should have been the best part—totally into Miranda.

And that was the problem. Yes, it was great to be adored, but it wasn't enough. Because when she looked at him, all Miranda could think was: *Yeah, he's okay.*

As they walked toward the coffee shop together, he took her hand—and she let him. It wasn't unpleasant, it was just—neutral. *Maybe this is how it's supposed to be,* she told herself. Girl likes boy, boy likes girl—maybe the sparks come later. Maybe love at first sight is for suckers and Hilary Duff movies. Maybe, out in the real world, being smart and nice and funny and kind of cute was enough. No wild heartbeats, no movie-star good looks, no rapt gazing into each other's eyes—just good food, good conversation . . . and an okay time.

That's what she told herself, at least, as they strolled through the night hand in hand. And she was almost convinced. Then they stepped inside the coffee shop.

And there he was.

Movie star good looks.

Her heart beating wildly.

Her gaze drawn inexorably to his.

Kane. And in an instant, she remembered what it was to feel, to want, to crave the touch of someone's hands, his lips, to glow under the warmth of his smile, to light up when he was around, to suddenly forget the existence of everyone else in the room. In the world. To look at other girls, foolish girls, and think, *How can they not see what I see?*

There was one guy in that room who made Miranda catch her breath with desire—and it wasn't the one she'd come in with.

He sat at a table with Harper and Kaia. (It was only later that it would occur to her to wonder what Harper—supposedly home studying—was doing out with Kane, or what either of them was doing with Kaia, of all people. But that was later.)

"Miranda!" Kane called out, catching sight of her and Greg and waving them over.

Miranda pulled Greg over to the table to say hello. She tried not to drool.

"Small world," she commented.

"Small *town*," Kaia snorted, and excused herself to get more sugar for her, as she put it, "sorry excuse for a macchiato."

"What are you guys doing here?" Miranda asked.

Harper shot Kane a cryptic look. "Study break," she said quickly. Then she noticed what Miranda was wearing, and her eyes widened in surprise. "That shirt—I thought—when did you get it?"

Miranda did a little twirl. "You like?"

"It's . . ."

"It's ravishing," Kane said with an approving grin. "No offense to your date here, but you keep dressing like that and he's going to have himself some serious competition."

Miranda flushed with pleasure. It was the first time Kane had ever given her a compliment on how she looked—maybe the outfit had done its job. Maybe Kane would finally start seeing her in a new light, as more than just a snarky brainiac. Or maybe Harper was right, and seeing her with another guy had made him jealous and—

Oh, right. Another guy.

She suddenly remembered Greg, who was standing quietly, obediently beside her. Shit.

They'd decided on coffee instead of alcohol, since Kane had a long night of Photoshopping ahead of him. And it had seemed a fine choice—until Miranda and her date walked in. Harper almost spat out her mochaccino at the site of her. In *that* outfit. Fortunately, it seemed Miranda was too dazzled by Kane's presence to wonder what the trio was doing there together. That was the silver lining— the black cloud, of course, was that Harper could tell from the queasy look on Miranda's face that this Greg thing wasn't going to work.

Not a big surprise—Greg was scrawny, gawky, and worst of all, bland. Under normal circumstances, Harper would have given him the big thumbs down—Miranda could do way better.

But these weren't normal circumstances, and she was going to have to take what Miranda could get. Which, at the moment, was a geeky, gawky loser. That, however, was a problem for another time—for tomorrow. Tonight she was still riding high on her triumph, and once Miranda was gone, she could continue celebrating in peace.

As Kane and Kaia bantered flirtatiously back and forth about who had the hottest drink, Harper zoned out, letting the conversation wash over her. The plan was set in motion now, and it was only a matter of time before the big pay-off. She didn't know how she was going to make it through the next couple days, hoping that nothing went wrong, that no one—including herself—lost their nerve, and knowing that by the end of the week, if all went according to plan, she and Adam would finally be together. And when that happened, she knew, she would stop all this ridiculous worrying about what she'd done and who she'd betrayed—because being with Adam would feel so right, it would jus-tify anything that had happened along the way. She couldn't wait.

Kane lifted his mug and proposed a toast.

"To getting what we want," he proclaimed, "by any means possible."

They clinked glasses and drank up. Harper smiled weakly, suddenly glad he hadn't suggested an alternate toast: "To getting what we deserve."

"Can you guys just shut up for one second?" Beth screamed in frustration. But it was no use. Her bratty brothers continued their hyperactive race through the house, hollering and squealing as they clomped up and down the stairs. Disaster was inevitable. Whether it would be one of the twins colliding with a heavy piece of furni-ture or Beth's head exploding (or some combination of the two, featuring an irate babysitter and a blunt object), she didn't know. But she did know she couldn't take this much longer. The stress of the SATs always looming over her, the fight she'd had with Adam eating away at her, and now, these brats. The world was conspiring to drive her insane.

Not that she didn't love her little brothers.

And maybe, if their house had been fully stocked with all that stuff supposed to keep five-year-olds in check—PlayStation, cable TV, DVD collection—she wouldn't have minded spending day after day after day with them. But her family couldn't afford any of that stuff. So the twins just had Beth—and each other. Normally, Adam would be here, occupying the twins with one of those lame magic tricks they loved, or teaching them how to tie different kinds of knots. Adam was an only child, and always claimed he was jealous of her "adorable" little brothers. "If you think they're so cute," Beth usually responded, "take them home with you. Please." But she had to admit that, when Adam was around, even *she* found her brothers kind of cute—he brought something out in them. And in himself.

But she and Adam weren't speaking to each other—hadn't since the day before, when he'd left her in the middle of the highway and sped away, covering her in a cloud of dust. She was on her own with the babysitting thing tonight, and that meant she had two options: continue to yell and scream, which would neither get the twins to shut up nor get her any closer to that perfect score—or bribe them with ice cream sundaes.

As always, it worked like a charm. Jeff and Sam, who, when they were silent, looked almost cherubic with their big blue eyes and curly blond hair, sat side by side at the table in front of their heaping bowls of ice cream, chocolate sauce, and a cherry for each. Their legs dangled several inches from the floor, swinging back and forth as they dug into their frozen treasure.

"Bethie, can I ask you a question?" Jeff asked, slurping down a spoonful of Rocky Road.

"Sure," she said, expecting to have to explain why the sky was blue or why Daddy smelled strange and acted so funny when he came home late at night.

"Is Kane your boyfriend now?"

"What? No, of course not," she said quickly. Kane had been over at the house a lot lately, studying—but she hadn't realized that her brothers had noticed.

"He's just a friend."

"I like him," Jeff said.

"Me too," Beth replied.

"But I like Adam better."

"Adam stinks, I like Kane," Sam countered. Beth knew he was just trying to get a rise out of his brother—but still, it hurt to hear.

"Sam, take that back!" she scolded him.

"No way," Sam said, grinning, seeing he'd made her mad. "Adam stinks. Kane's way better."

"Adam is!" Jeff yelled.

"No, Kane!"

They went back and forth, louder and louder, until finally Beth pulled away both their ice cream dishes and held them high in the air.

"No more, unless you guys behave!" she threatened.

They shut up immediately, and she handed back the bowls.

"But Beth," Sam asked quietly, "which one do *you* like better?"

They both stared at her, their eyes filled with curiosity, and Beth shifted uncomfortably in her seat. It was just too weird to hear the question coming out of her little brother's mouth, the same question that Adam had been pestering her with one way or another for weeks. The same question that kept bouncing up in her mind no matter how hard and how many times she tried to push it away.

"I like them *both*, Sam, in different ways."

"But who do you like *better*?" Jeff repeated insistently.

She ignored the question and skipped over to the refrigerator. When in doubt, distract.

"We almost forgot—who wants whipped cream!"

Greg pulled the car to a stop in front of Miranda's house.

"So," he said awkwardly, turning off the ignition and staring straight ahead as if afraid to look at her.

"So," she repeated, giving him a half smile. Part of her wanted to throw open the door, jump out of the car and never look back. But it would be so rude, even cruel . . . and a part of her was just a little curious to see what would happen if she stayed.

So she did.

"I had a great time tonight," he said hopefully, twining his fingers with hers.

"Me too," she replied—it was only polite. She looked down at her hand, linked with his, as if it belonged to someone else.

He touched her cheek with his other hand. "I'm really glad you agreed to go out with me."

He was so earnest, it was painful. "You've got really pretty eyes," he whispered. "You know that?"

Oh God, just kiss me already, she thought, stifling a laugh. But she just smiled sweetly. "Thanks."

And then, even though she'd been waiting for it, he took her by surprise. One moment his face was a foot away, the next it was on hers, bumping awkwardly against her nose, and then their lips were suctioned together. There was no wave of passion, not even a ripple. Instead, she just observed, as if from very far away.

His lips were oddly soft and very wet.

She'd never before noticed how strange kissing was, really. All that squishing and sucking and smacking together. Where your tongue goes and what your hands should be doing. She'd never really thought about it before.

But then, she supposed, you probably weren't supposed to be thinking very much, during. You certainly weren't supposed to be thinking about your unfinished chem lab or yesterday's episode of *General Hospital* while his fingers were crawling up beneath your shirt, hungrily grasping at your bare skin. And you probably shouldn't be thinking about another guy.

But Miranda was—and wished that those were his arms wrapped around her, his breath hot against her neck.

But then again—

It was dark inside the car, and they were just shadowy silhouettes pressed against each other. He could be anyone. She could be anyone. When she closed her eyes, there was only the feel of a body next to hers, of a solid chest and broad shoulders, of warm flesh and hard muscle.

When she closed her eyes, they were two strangers coming together in the dark.

When she closed her eyes—he could be anyone.

chapter

11

"So I think I'm going to ditch out on this whole swim meet thing," Miranda said, stretching herself out on Harper's living room couch.

"What do you mean, 'ditch out'?" Harper asked lazily. She was curled up in a worn orange armchair, feeling far too relaxed and contented to get upset about Miranda's last-minute change of heart. "Why wouldn't you go?"

"I don't know." Miranda, who'd been playing a game of 'should I or shouldn't I eat this' with a bag of Chips Ahoy! for the last twenty minutes, finally pushed the unopened bag away in disgust. "With the SATs and all, it just seems like maybe I should stay home and study—"

"The SATs aren't until Saturday," Harper pointed out. "We'll get back from Valley Glen Thursday night—you'll have all day Friday to study." They'd had this conversation already, a few days before, and Harper had thought the matter was closed.

"Yeah, but I'll be totally wiped, and it's probably better if I—"

"Miranda, what's *really* going on?" Harper interrupted, shaking her head. It's not like Miranda's presence on Thursday was at all crucial to the plan—but she didn't like last-minute changes, not this late in the game. Not when everything was moving along so perfectly.

Miranda flushed and looked away. "I just think it'll be weird," she admitted. "Greg's going, and I don't want to . . . I think it's better if I just stick around here. I'm sure I can find someone who wants to do some last-minute cramming." She laughed ruefully. "There's always Beth—I'm sure she's not going anywhere two days before the SATs, and—" Miranda suddenly caught a glimpse of Harper's face, which had almost completely drained of color. "What?"

But Harper was struck speechless for a moment, as she felt her whole plan begin to unravel.

"Just to avoid this guy Greg, you'd stay home and"— she could barely bring herself to say it—"study with *Beth*?"

"Well, I was kind of joking about the Beth thing," Miranda allowed, "but actually, it doesn't seem like the worst idea in the world."

"Except that it is," Harper countered heatedly—and then caught herself. She couldn't have Miranda staying home and screwing everything up. She couldn't leave Beth with a potential alibi. But what was she supposed to tell Miranda?

Obviously not the truth.

"So exactly what was so wrong with this guy?" Harper asked, stalling for time as she desperately tried to figure out how to get Miranda on that bus and safely out of town.

"There was nothing *wrong* with him," Miranda clarified, sounding exasperated. "I just don't think I need to be with a guy I'm not really that into."

"Okay, *first* of all, hooking up in a car does not qualify as being 'with' him, so just take it easy. Second of all, you've only been on one date—that's, what, four hours? You have no way of knowing whether you're into him or not." Harper cringed at her own words, since she'd only needed thirty seconds with Greg to determine he was a loser. But in principle, she reasoned, it was sound advice. So what if she and Miranda, experts in snap judgment, had never followed it before? There was a first time for everything.

"I know that when I stood him next to Kane, it wasn't pretty. Doesn't it seem like the guy you're with—excuse me, on a date with—should at least seem like the most appealing guy in the room?"

Uh, not when you have no chance in hell of getting the one you really want, Harper thought. But she couldn't say that.

"Miranda, you know that old song, 'If you can't be with the one you love, love the one you're with'?" she said instead.

"No, and if you start singing, I'm walking out right now."

"No singing, I promise. Just a suggestion—give the guy another chance. Forget you ever saw Kane last night."

"What were you all doing there, anyway?" Miranda asked suspiciously. "I thought you were staying in."

"Oh?" Well, at least this time she'd known it was coming, and she'd had some time to prepare. "Yeah—uh, Kane told me he was going out with Kaia to talk about . . . their history project, and I invited myself along. You know, to keep an eye on him—for you!" *You are an evil person—and, all of a sudden, a shitty liar,* she told herself. She hoped Miranda would buy it.

"Well, thanks, I guess," Miranda said grudgingly. "I can't believe you were willing to subject yourself to a night with Kaia just to keep him away from her. For me."

"Well, believe it." *Please, please believe it.*

"So you *do* still think I've got a chance?" Miranda asked, her voice filled with a new hope.

It was a hope that Harper knew she should shoot down immediately, for Miranda's sake, if not for her own. But if she was going to get Miranda to this swim meet, Harper was going to need to use some bait. And she had just the thing.

"I think . . . it can't hurt to find out. And this whole swim team championship could be your perfect opportunity."

"Why—is Kane coming?"

"He's on the swim team, isn't he?" Harper replied carefully. It was a true statement . . . it just didn't actually answer the question. "You can spend some time with him, be there to support him. And as for Greg—how do you think Kane will feel, seeing some guy chasing after *you* for a change?"

"I don't know if it's such a good idea, Harper," Miranda said dubiously. "Having the two of them side by side? It might not be—"

"I saw the way Kane was staring at you in that coffee shop, Rand," Harper broke in, throwing caution to the wind. "Seeing you with another guy? It made him look at you in a whole new way."

"I thought so too!" Miranda crowed.

Harper smiled weakly, feeling like a sticky gob of something you peel off the bottom of your shoe. It wouldn't be so bad, she told herself. Maybe once she spent some more time with this loser, Miranda would decide she actually liked him—maybe she'd finally forget all about Kane. When you thought about it, Harper was doing Miranda a service—Kane was a sleazebag, not good enough for her best friend. Things were bad enough now, with Miranda chasing after him so pathetically—but she'd be much, much worse off if she ever got what she wanted. Kane was bad news.

Miranda needed someone good, someone solid. Really, if she knew what Harper was up to, if she knew the *whole* story, she'd have to be grateful. She'd have to say thank you.

But maybe it was better not to risk it.

They arrived at the school at seven the next day, just after sunrise. The swim team, riding in a separate van, had already left, and Miranda and Harper found themselves lost amid a sea of rabid Haven High fans. It had been a long time since either of them had attended a school sporting event—now, trapped in a rowdy crowd of students waiting to get on the bus, they remembered why they'd stayed away.

"Miranda! Hey, over here!" The two girls looked over toward the sound of the voice to see a life-size foam cactus pushing through the crowd—and heading straight toward them. "Hey, I was hoping you'd be here," the cactus-guy called, bobbing his head awkwardly—thanks to the costume, his arms were both stuck rigidly out from his body, as if in a permanent double-handed wave.

"Do we know this loser?" Harper muttered to Miranda, as the cactus approached.

Miranda just sighed.

"Hi, Greg. When you said you were coming, you didn't mention you'd be—" She gestured to his elaborate green foam costume. It was too horrible for words.

"I'm the mascot," he explained, a wide smile breaking out on his face. "I'm supposed to bring some cheer for the cheering section."

"Well you certainly brought *us* some morning cheer," Harper said snidely, smirking at Miranda.

Miranda just sneered back—then yelped in dismay as Greg's thorny arm wrapped around her and pulled her toward the bus.

"Our chariot awaits, madame," he told her gallantly. "You can help me lead the fight song."

Harper stifled a laugh and tried her best to ignore the pleading look in Miranda's eyes as Greg dragged her away. She knew she should probably feel guilty, but she couldn't help it: All she felt was a rush of anticipation and excitement, and the warm certainty that everything was finally falling into place, exactly as she'd planned.

She found a seat for herself on the bus and watched out the window as they pulled out of the lot and onto the open road. The road stretched ahead of them, and Grace soon fell behind—and as the miles wore on, her heart grew lighter and lighter. It was all going to work. By the time the bus returned to Grace, late that night, everything would be different. And Harper would have everything she'd ever wanted. It felt like she'd been waiting a lifetime; but only a few hours more, and her wait would finally be over.

✧✧✧

The pit stop was, almost literally, a pit.

It was a gas station in the middle of nowhere, a lonely gray outpost in the gray desert landscape. It looked abandoned, a wreck of a building that faded into the washed-out sepia tones of the scrub-brush covered land. But after three hours on the road, cramped together in a tiny van with nothing but drab scenery, dirty jokes, and a scratched-up Outkast CD to keep them entertained, the swim team was ready for a break. And they weren't picky.

Besides, at least there was a bathroom—unisex, and looking as if it had only recently been introduced to indoor plumbing, but semifunctional nonetheless. There was a small convenience store area by the cash register, where the coffee looked like it should have been dispensed by the ancient, rust-encrusted gas pumps, but it was coffee.

And there was even cell reception. Just in one spot, behind the semi-outhouse and a few feet from where the owner had tethered a sallow, swaybacked horse, but one spot was all Adam needed.

He couldn't do it, couldn't leave town without at least *trying* to talk things out with Beth. Or rather, he *had* left town, without saying a word, and it was killing him. He would go no farther.

"Hello? Beth?" he shouted when she picked up the phone, trying to make himself heard through the static.

"Adam? Is that you?"

"Beth?" He could barely hear her.

"Where *are* you?" she asked, her voice punctuated by static and silence. "You're cutting in and out."

"Beth, I wanted to apologize." It took a great deal of

effort to get the words out—since really, it was the last thing he wanted to do.

"What? You want to what?"

"I'm sorry!" he shouted.

"Did you say you can't hear me? I can't hear you, either."

"Beth, I just want to . . ."

She interrupted, but her response was incomprehensible. There was too much static, too many moments of dead air.

"Adam, I—you, but you—if—and then Kane—"

"What? What about Kane?"

"—have to go, Adam—later?"

"Beth, wait!" he called uselessly.

Disconnected.

"Nervous?" Harper asked, hoping that her voice sounded normal and that Adam wouldn't notice the desire throbbing beneath her carefully casual smile. They stood at the edge of the Olympic-size pool, waiting for Adam's heat to start, and as Adam shifted his weight from one foot to the other and anxiously watched his teammates finish up the butterfly relay, Harper watched . . . Adam.

He was wearing nothing but tight orange briefs and an orange and black swim cap with goggles strapped around his head. His tan skin glistened, still wet from his warm-up laps. Harper's eyes traced a path down his taut biceps, his chiseled abs, the angular curves of his muscles. . . . His body was like a work of art.

"Not really," he murmured, looking out at the huge crowd of screaming spectators. "It's just a meet, just like any other."

The lie was obvious in his face, but Harper didn't call him on it.

"Good," she said warmly. "Nothing to be nervous about."

He looked past her into the distance for a moment, a wistful look crossing his face.

"I just wish . . ." His voice trailed off, but Harper knew what he was thinking. He wished that Beth were there. Sweet, loving Beth, his little good luck charm, always there to support him in his time of need. But she wasn't there now, was she?

Better get used to it, she warned him silently.

"Never mind," he said, shaking it off. "It's going to be fine. I'm going to be fine."

"You're going to be *great,*" she corrected him—and suddenly, without fearing what he would do or think, threw her arms around him. *Just a friendly hug,* she told herself, pretending not to notice the warm touch of his bare skin against her body. *For now.* "Good luck," she murmured.

"Thanks, Harper," he whispered, clutching her tightly. "I'm glad you're here."

So was she.

Adam loved swimming. He loved the way his body sliced through the water, he loved the harsh, unforgiving rhythm of the strokes, and he loved the feel of his muscles working in concert, disconnected from his mind, from worries of speed or victory, just pushing and pushing, toward their limit. And, on good days, beyond.

But most of all, he loved the silence. When he dove off

the edge and slipped beneath the water, the noise of the world dropped away. The screams and cheers of the crowd disappeared, and the universe narrowed to a single bluish tunnel of water. Nothing mattered except his body and his breathing, and forcing his limbs to cut through the water, surging ever ahead. He could shut out all the background noise of his life, shut off his mind, and just focus. Just be.

But today, with so much riding on this race—and with so many problems waiting for him back on dry land—he worried that the water wouldn't work its familiar magic. As he stood poised at the edge of the pool, waiting for his moment, he couldn't get the noise to stop, couldn't find his focus. It wasn't just the screaming crowd, or the yells of his teammates. It was the sound of Beth's voice in his head, telling him she wouldn't be there. Telling him she'd rather stay home, with Kane. Faces flashed through his head: an apologetic Beth, a smirking Kane, and then Harper, with such a look of calm and comfort that he almost believed her, for a moment, that everything would be okay. At the thought of Harper, the voices almost quieted, and the rapid pounding of Adam's heart subsided—but only for a moment. Because thinking of Harper cheering for him on the sidelines reminded him of Beth's absence. And that led him back to Kane. He couldn't escape it, the sound of his own thoughts and fears. He couldn't clear his mind, couldn't concentrate, and then—

The sharp report of the starting gun.

A dive off the edge, the sharp pain of cold water slamming into him.

A new world, silent and awash in blue.

His mind shut down, his body took over—and Adam finally let go.

✧✧✧

They'd had a marathon study day, cramming last-minute vocab and equations into their heads for hours on end until even Beth felt like her brain was about to melt.

"I'm totally burnt," she finally said, throwing down her pen. "How about a break? We can pick up with this again in the morning."

"You?" Kane asked with mock incredulity. "My faithful taskmaster is actually suggesting we stop early? How *inconceivable!*"

"Hey, I can be *stupefying* sometimes."

They both burst into laughter at the ridiculously unnecessary use of SAT words.

"God, we have turned into complete SAT nerds, haven't we?" Beth moaned through her laughter.

"Harvard, here I come." He looked serious suddenly. "And it's all thanks to you."

"Oh, no, Kane," she said, blushing. "I don't even know why you wanted my help in the first place—you're such a quick study. I barely had to do anything."

"You did plenty," he insisted. "And I still can't believe you were willing to waste so much time on a screwup like me, not when you had so much else you needed to take care of."

"It was my pleasure," Beth assured him. "What would I have done without the company?"

They sat across the table from each other, silent for a moment. The air was charged with tension. Beth stared into his eyes, wanted to look away, but couldn't. She didn't know what she was doing or feeling—but she knew it was dangerous.

"Well, I don't know about you," she said finally, with a forced joviality intended to break the intensity of the moment. Her too-loud voice seemed to echo in the still room. "But I'm *voraciously ravenous*. You want to meet back here early tomorrow?"

Kane smiled. "Actually, I think I've got a better idea—meet me at the northeast corner of Dwyer Park in an hour? I've got a little surprise for you."

"Tonight? Don't you have a hot date or something?" She winced inwardly at the thought of him groping yet another bimbo—or worse, someone actually substantive, someone he could really fall for.

She stopped herself, suddenly—that wouldn't be worse, that would be *better*. She wanted the best for Kane, she reminded herself. He should be with someone good, someone substantive—someone else.

"There's nowhere I'd rather be tonight than with you," he assured her. "Now, I know I'm only a poor stand-in for Adam—"

"Forget about Adam," she said, a little more harshly than she'd intended. "You're right. We've been working hard, and we deserve to celebrate—you and me."

"Okay, then don't forget," he said, heading toward the door. "Dwyer Park, northeast corner, one hour. Can't wait."

Neither could she.

Adam raised his trophy over his head one more time, and the Haven High fans sent up a deafening cheer. He'd been grinning so hard, and for so long, that his face felt stretched out of shape, but he couldn't stop. Third place in the four-hundred-yard IM at regional championships—it was better than he'd ever expected to do. And if he was disappointed to have lost out on first place by only a few seconds—well, his beaming teammates and the adoring crowd had wiped such thoughts from his mind.

He turned to Harper, who'd been standing loyally by his side all day long. She'd been there to wish him luck before his races, and had greeted him with a howl of triumph every time he'd pulled himself out of the pool. After his big event, the four-hundred IM, he'd swept her, soaking wet, into a tight hug—relieved the race was over, relieved he had someone with whom to share his victory. Together, they'd watched the rest of the heats, cheered on his teammates, waited through the interminable award ceremony. And when Adam had stood to receive his two-foot-high trophy, Harper's shouts of encouragement had risen above the noise of the crowd.

The meet had cleared his mind, worn him out. He had no energy, no will, to think about his problems, to worry—instead he just relaxed and enjoyed himself. And enjoyed Harper. It was so easy between the two of them. They'd been friends for so long that they didn't have to *try* when they were together, they didn't have to wonder or worry about what the other was thinking. They could just laugh and talk—just be together.

"Come on," he urged her, throwing an arm around her shoulders and pulling her along. Now that the meet was over, the hosting high school was throwing a big, all-school pizza party—and he wanted to get there before all the pepperoni was gone.

Harper leaned against his shoulder and smiled up at

him, and Adam marveled for a moment at the warmth and sincerity that filled her eyes. He knew there were a lot of people at Haven High who had their doubts about Harper—but if they only knew her like he knew her . . .

"Actually," she hedged, giving him a mischievous grin, "I have a better idea."

As she explained, Adam laughed and shook his head—leave it to Harper to find her Valley Glen equivalent and snag an invitation to the Pit, a secluded clearing in the nearby woods that was apparently *the* place to hang, if you were into that whole good music, warm beer, no adult supervision thing. (And who wasn't?)

"She promises it's better than it sounds," Harper wheedled. "A bunch of them are headed over there now—"

"We don't even know these people," Adam said hesitantly. "And you don't want to miss the bus."

"It's close by—we'll be back with plenty of time to spare," she promised, pressing closer to him. "No one will even notice we're gone."

Adam shrugged his shoulders and nodded. He supposed that he should stick around for the pizza thing, bond with his teammates—but suddenly, laughing it up with the guys, watching them stuff their faces with pizza and smash soda cans against their foreheads, didn't have much appeal. Not compared to sneaking off somewhere mellow and secluded, somewhere with Harper.

Besides, at this point Adam would have agreed to pretty much anything. He felt strange—weirdly relaxed, loose. It took him a moment to place the unfamiliar sensation, but then he got it: He was happy.

✧✧✧

Beth didn't know what to expect when she walked up to the park—really a dusty brown square in the middle of town with a sprinkling of sallow, brittle grass that the town replanted, to no avail, every winter, only to see it all die off by the end of summer. There was a rickety band shell at the other end, which tonight was festooned with banners advertising: GRACE NOTES IN CONCERT! ONE NIGHT ONLY! She smiled and shook her head. This town got more ridiculous with every passing day.

When she found Kane, he waved and, with a flourish, pulled a daisy from behind his back.

"What's this?" she asked, giggling.

"A flower for the lady," he said. "Just the beginning—follow me, please." He led her through the park toward a picnic blanket that was laid out with a cornucopia of delicious-looking food—heaping sandwiches, cheese, fresh-baked bread, chocolate-covered strawberries, and a bottle of red wine in the center. Kane sat down and gestured for her to do the same.

"You did all this?" she asked, eyes wide.

"I'm a man of many talents," he said, pouring her a glass of wine. "I figured it was the least I could do to thank you."

"It's amazing," she breathed. And it was: the food, the warm breeze, the starry sky. "This is just what I needed—how did you know?"

"Like you said, I'm a quick study. But that's not all." He looked at his watch. "The entertainment portion of our evening should be starting just . . . about . . . now—"

Suddenly a low base line began booming out of the speaker propped up a few feet behind them, and a moment later a four-part harmony broke into the familiar strains of "Blue Moon," one of Beth's favorite oldies.

She looked up at the band shell and, sure enough, four old men in silver vests and bowler hats—the Grace Notes, she assumed—were crooning away. In the darkness Beth could barely see any of the other picnickers, and it felt like they were singing just to her.

"Did you know about this?" she asked Kane.

"I saw the fliers earlier this week," he admitted. "Thought it could be fun."

"I wouldn't think this was quite your speed," she told him, laughing—she'd been laughing so much these past few weeks.

"Hey, we can leave if you want," he offered, starting to get up.

"Leave? Are you crazy?" She grabbed his arm and pulled him back down again, taking a sip from the glass of wine. She almost never drank—but this was, after all, a special occasion. The wine trickled down her throat, warm, sweet, and delicious. "This is wonderful, Kane—thank you." She leaned over and hugged him. For just a moment too long.

They sat side by side in the moonlight, enjoying the food and the wine, letting the music wash over them, laughing, talking—and then, as the night wore on, quiet. And close.

And when Beth's cell phone rang, she didn't answer it—didn't even check to see if it might be Adam.

And when she shivered, and Kane slowly, tentatively put an arm around her and pulled her close to his warm body, she didn't move away.

chapter

12

Adam came back to the small campfire and plopped down next to Harper, who passed him a joint. "Everything okay?" she asked quietly.

Adam, who didn't usually go for pot, inhaled deeply and hoped that if it was going to mellow him out, it would work fast.

"Fine," he said shortly.

He didn't know why he'd had to ruin a perfectly good day. He'd been in a great mood, tired but happy—so he'd let his guard down, called Beth to share the good news of his victory.

There was no answer.

Was she screening? Was she out?

He didn't know, and he supposed it didn't matter. What mattered was that he was here now, free, and if he didn't stop stressing, the moment was going to pass him by.

He looked good-naturedly around at the small group

of Valley Glen high schoolers who'd gathered at the Pit. Their names and faces may have been different from the familiar Haven High crowd, but they seemed familiar— Adam had never felt so instantly at home. An old Jay-Z album was booming through the tinny speakers of an old boombox, and Adam leaned his head back, enjoying the way the driving beat enlivened the still, dark woods. He and Harper were perched on a thick log in front of the improvised campfire, next to Miranda and her new guy, who had tagged along when Harper and Adam sneaked away from the pizza bash. It was just like being back in Grace—only better, because here Adam wasn't the center of attention, wasn't the big man on campus, carrying the burden of everyone's hopes and expectations. Here he could just sit back and watch the action from the sidelines.

"I'm glad you dragged me out here," he confided to Harper in a low voice, leaning close to her ear.

She favored him with a warm grin. "Me too, Ad."

Suddenly filled with a burst of affection and gratitude for his oldest friend, he swept her into a bear hug.

"What would I do without you, Gracie?" It was what he'd called her sometimes when they were kids, because it was funny to watch her get red in the face and throw things at him. He knew she secretly loved it.

"Good thing you'll never have to find out," she promised him in a muffled voice.

"Dude, get a room!" one of the random Valley Glen guys called out.

Adam looked up, suddenly realizing everyone was looking at him. Maybe he wasn't the center of attention out here—but he wasn't invisible, either. He flushed hotly and jumped up. "You guys think we need more beer?" he asked Harper and Miranda. "I think we need more beer. I'll go grab some." He jogged off in the direction of the massive coolers.

No one here knew him, of course—and it seemed unlikely that Miranda or her random guy would run home and start spreading gossip. And, Adam reminded himself, there was nothing to gossip about—he and Harper were just friends. Everyone knew that. But still, if someone got the wrong idea, and somehow Beth got wind of it . . . that was really all he needed, for word to get back to Beth that he'd been up here macking on Harper.

On the other hand . . . he pictured her and Kane back in town together, curled up on a couch, studying, ignoring her ringing phone. Maybe she wouldn't even care.

And maybe he didn't either.

"Can I talk to you for a second?" Miranda hissed as soon as Adam was gone. It wasn't a request.

"What is it?" Harper asked, visibly annoyed.

She was annoyed? Let her try spending the day fending off the advances of a *human cactus* who had all the sexual chemistry of a rock. *Then* she could talk to Miranda about feeling annoyed.

"Not here," she whispered, and dragged Harper off deeper into the woods, away from the rest of the group—away from Greg. "I cannot believe you," she told Harper, once they were a safe distance away from the group.

"What?" Harper asked wearily.

"What do you mean, 'what'? What's the deal with telling Greg we were coming out here and inviting him along? Like I didn't have enough trouble staying away from him all day long?"

"I don't know," Harper mused, "he's kind of cute without the cactus outfit. Aren't you having fun?"

"No, that would be *you*," Miranda said slowly. "We're talking about *me* now—something I know you have some trouble wrapping your brain around."

"What's that supposed to mean?"

"It means you dragged me along on this stupid trip, when I could have been home studying—and now I'm stuck out here in the middle of nowhere while you and Adam gaze into each other's eyes and Greg tries to stuff his hand down my shirt."

"Well, that's why I invited Greg along," Harper pointed out defensively. "To keep you company. Besides, you didn't have to come. I told you that you could stay for the pizza thing. We could have met up later."

"Right, like I was going to spend the night with those mindless drones. I *thought* we were going to be hanging out together."

"So here we are," Harper pointed out, "together. What are you complaining about?"

She just wasn't getting it. But she would.

"I don't know, maybe about the fact that you totally lured me out here under false pretenses," Miranda snapped. "Or have you forgotten your little plan," she lowered her voice to a whisper, "to make Kane jealous? Somehow, I don't think it's going to work—because, gosh," Miranda widened her eyes and craned her neck around in exaggerated confusion. "I don't see him *anywhere*, do you?"

"Very funny. Like I knew he was going to pull a no-show? Besides, is your life all about Kane now? Wherever he goes, you follow?"

"That's not the point, Harper, and you know it. The point is that you suckered me into coming up here, then ignored me all day, and stuck me with . . . *the mascot*. Do you know what people must be thinking when they see us together?"

"So that's all you care about now?" Harper asked. "He's not good enough for you? And I thought I was supposed to be the shallow one."

Miranda recoiled—maybe because, deep down, she recognized a sliver of truth in Harper's words. Greg was sweet, funny—but he'd spent the day acting like the court jester, not caring that everyone was laughing at him. Maybe he didn't mind being the center of ridicule, but Miranda wasn't looking to become Mrs. Class Clown anytime soon. Still, Harper, of all people, had no right to accuse her—not now, not after today.

"Did you ever think that maybe I just don't like spending time with some guy who's chasing after me when I know I'm not interested?" she asked.

"Did it ever occur to you that I'm doing you a favor?" Harper retorted.

"Oh?"

"Maybe if you give this guy a chance, instead of chasing after something you can't have, you could actually be *happy* for once. Though I know that would just screw with your whole view of the universe."

Miranda snapped. Harper had deceived her, ditched her—and now, instead of apologizing, was acting like Miranda was making the whole thing up? Just looking for an excuse to complain? Miranda had been the model friend—always there when Harper needed her, always ready to support her wild ideas, sympathize with her ridiculous problems. And what did she ask for in return? Not much: a little companionship, a little understanding. What did she get? Nothing. No, worse—she got an endless day with dull-as-dirt Greg, while Harper did what she wanted, as usual, with no apologies and apparently no regrets. Because things were different for Harper, right? Because she played with a different set of rules.

That had always been the understanding, at least—and Miranda was fed up.

"Look who's talking!" Miranda yelled. "I'm not the one chasing after a guy who's already got a girlfriend. And is totally in love with her. You want to talk to me about pathetic and hopeless?"

"That's different," Harper said hotly.

"Why? Because you're Harper Grace and you always get what you want? And meanwhile I'm supposed to settle for second-best?"

"That's not what I said."

"But it's what you meant. It's what you always mean. But why? Why should I have to settle for someone I think is just okay? Why can't I hold out for something that's really amazing? Don't you think I *deserve* something amazing?"

"Of course you do, Rand," Harper said sincerely.

"Then why the hell does everyone always want me to *settle*?"

"I don't," said a low, male voice behind them.

They spun around to see Greg standing a couple feet

away. He'd obviously heard everything—or, at least, enough.

"I just came to see if everything was all right," he explained awkwardly.

Miranda took a step toward him. "Greg—," she began in a faltering voice, but broke off, not sure what to say.

"No, I get it," he told her, his face impassive—but it was obviously taking him a great deal of effort to keep it that way. "You don't want to settle—that's fair. You think you deserve better." He shrugged and bit down on his lower lip. "So do I."

And he walked away, back toward the school.

Miranda and Harper stood frozen in place for a moment, and then tears began leaking down Miranda's face.

"I can't believe he—Harper, I feel so terrible, and he—" She stopped, her voice choked off by sobs, and Harper wrapped her in a tight hug.

"I'm a terrible person," Miranda whimpered.

"No, you're not," Harper assured her.

"I'm going to be alone forever—I deserve to be alone forever."

"No you don't, Rand. Look, here's what I think. You just need to—"

She was stopped by the sound of her cell phone ringing. They both looked down at the caller ID—Kaia.

"Why's she calling you?" Miranda asked.

But Harper had already answered the phone.

"Kaia? Can we do this later? Or—no, okay, I understand. Just give me a sec."

She took the phone away from her ear. "Miranda, I have to take this," she said lamely. "I'm sorry."

Tears still streaming down her face, Miranda looked at her best friend in shock.

"You're kidding, right? You're going to leave me here so you can talk to *Kaia*?"

Harper looked confused for a moment, then looked away.

"I'm sorry, I just have to." She gave Miranda another hug, but Miranda pulled away.

"This won't take long," Harper promised. "I'll meet you back by the fire, and we'll talk the whole thing out. I swear."

"Whatever." Miranda turned away, her shoulders shaking. "Have fun talking to Kaia. Tell her I say hello," she added bitterly.

Harper didn't respond, and when Miranda finally turned around, she was gone.

Harper hurried back to the clearing and knelt by Adam's side, handing him her cell. "Adam, there's a call on my phone that I think you need to take," she whispered urgently.

"What? What do you mean?" He looked at the phone in confusion.

Harper pulled him away from the campfire and led him off into the woods, away from everyone, stopping when they'd reached a cluster of low-hanging trees.

"Just trust me, it's important—something you're going to want to hear."

She left him alone and, bewildered, Adam put the phone to his ear. The reception was shockingly clear.

"Hello?"

"Adam, it's Kaia."

"Kaia? Jesus, what the hell are you calling me for? And on Harper's phone?"

"Adam, don't hang up—please. This is serious."

She sounded desperate and, against his better judgment, he took his finger off the end button. For the moment.

"You've got one minute—talk," he said gruffly.

"I don't know how to tell you this," she began hesitantly. "I went into school today—it was open, you know, and I wanted to do some laps in the pool, and, well, I didn't think there'd be anyone else there, but—"

She stopped.

"Spit it out," he ordered.

"They were there when I came in," she said haltingly. "In the locker room. All over each other."

"Who?" But he thought he knew. A hollow space opened inside of him as he waited for the words to be spoken aloud, to make it real.

"Beth and Kane."

There it was. Three syllables. Funny that it took so little to ruin everything.

"And I'm supposed to believe that? From *you*, of all people?" He wanted to believe she was lying—but couldn't. He was the one who'd been lying, to himself. All along, telling himself there was nothing to worry about. Stupid.

"Why would I lie about this, Adam? Look, I know I've treated you . . . poorly in the past."

He let out a barking laugh. *That* was the understatement of the year.

"But I have a lot of respect for you," she said, emotion filling her voice. "You don't deserve this."

"Kaia, I'm not throwing away a two-year relationship on your say so," he said hollowly.

"I thought you'd say that," she responded. "That's why I called on Harper's phone. It's camera-equipped—and I've got proof."

He looked at the phone's tiny view screen, and a moment later there they were, right in front of him—Beth and Kane, in each other's arms. Naked. Entangled.

The screen was tiny, the resolution poor, but he could make out Beth's hair, her face, the mole on her left shoulder blade. He could see her kissing Kane, rubbing his bare chest, letting him lick her neck and—he flipped the phone shut. Hanging up on Kaia, shutting out the nightmarish pictures. He'd known it was true, yes, but to *see* it?

The images were seared into his brain. He smashed his fist into the ground, a volcano of rage erupting within him. He slammed the phone into the ground as hard as he could and stomped on it, imagining it was Kane's neck he was crushing beneath his heavy boot.

"Adam, are you okay?" Harper asked tentatively, emerging from behind the trees.

"Go away, Harper," he said in a strangled voice. No one should see him like this.

"Adam?"

"I just need some time alone, okay? I just—please, Harper, go."

She nodded and backed away.

"You know where to find me when you need me," she promised.

Promises—what were they worth to him anymore? Adam sank onto the ground and laid his head in his hands. Was this his fault? Had he started it, sleeping with Kaia in the first place?

No.

A cold certainty filled him, a righteous rage—this was no one-time thing, no harmless fling. This was Beth, his Beth, so innocent, so trustworthy—*supposedly*—and Kane, his best friend, his bro, his loyal and true ally. This was an affair, a dirty, scummy, poisonous affair between two heartless traitors who'd betrayed him and everything he thought was real.

He wanted to scream.

He wanted to hit something, someone.

He wanted to cry.

But instead, he just sat there on the cold ground, immobile, silent.

It was all over now, all of it. There was nothing left.

When it became clear Adam had hung up on her, Kaia snapped the phone shut with a satisfied grin. He could deny it all he wanted, but she knew he'd believed her the moment the words were out of her mouth. He'd believed it before she even picked up the phone. The pictures were just gravy—but they'd definitely sealed the deal.

"Kaia, I'm getting bored in here. Why don't you come back to bed?" the languid, British voice called to her from the bedroom—where the handsome British man who owned it lay sprawled across his silk sheets, waiting for her.

"Be right there!" she called. "And I've got a surprise for you."

She stopped in the small kitchen and pulled a can of whipped cream and a jar of chocolate syrup out of the fridge. Powell always said he didn't like surprises, but this one would be too sweet to resist. She gave herself a quick once-over in the hallway mirror and then, turning off her phone and laying it on the counter, headed down the hall to begin her night for real.

I've done my part now, she thought, sending a telepathic message out toward Kane and Harper, who were about to reap the benefits of a carefully laid plan. *Your turn—just don't screw it up.*

Eventually, the anger had seeped out of him.

Or rather, the anger was still there, like acid, burning a hole deep inside of him, but all his energy had washed away, and he felt slow, heavy, weighed down by a deep sadness. And he knew then that he didn't want to be alone.

He walked back toward the Pit to find Harper—but she found him first. She was sitting on the ground by the side of the trail. Waiting for him.

"You're always there when I need you," he marveled, his voice breaking midway through the sentence.

"Oh, Adam," Harper moaned. "Kaia told me—I'm so sorry, I—"

"Please, stop," he said quietly. "Let's not—just stop."

A tear trickled down his face and she caught it with her fingertip as it rolled down his cheek, then pulled him into a hug. He leaned against her, crying silently in her arms, deeply ashamed, and knowing that there was no one, *no one* in the world he would allow to see him like this. No one but Harper. He leaned against her, and she held him up. Like always.

"I broke your cell phone," he murmured into her hair.

"I don't care about that," she said, pulling back and looking him in the eye. "I care about you." She gently pressed her hand against his cheek. "Let's take a walk," she suggested. "I think you need some air."

She put an arm around him and led him down the forest trail and away from the pit. They walked in silence, past the silhouetted trees and shadows cast by looming rock formations. The night was bright, the moonlight filtering in through a canopy of leaves. At the edge of the woods they turned to make sure the Grace bus and van were still there, silently waiting in the parking lot. Then they walked along the perimeter of the woods, listening to the whispering wind and the distant howling of a coyote.

Adam, lost in a world of his own thoughts and regrets, noticed none of it.

Finally, Harper led them over to a square, flat rock that lay tucked between a cluster of saplings.

"Just like our rock," she said, scrambling up onto it and pulling him after her. They lay back on the cool granite and stared up at the sky—and she was right, it did feel for a moment like they were back home, in the backyard, a million years ago, when it had been just the two of them and everything had been so simple.

His mind dipped through the past, skidding across memories of long-ago days. So many moments that had brought him to this one. And Harper—he turned his head to look at her and realized she was staring at him, eyes awash in love and sympathy—Harper had been there for almost all of them. She was the one constant in his life. His father gone, his mother useless, his girlfriend and his best friend—

No, there was only Harper. Loyal. True. Just thinking about her, just lying there so close to her made the anger subside, made the world seem almost bearable, made the red tide of pain and betrayal recede.

She reached over and took his hand, squeezing it gently, and he squeezed back, then shifted onto his side and looked at her. For the first time, *really* looked at her. And realized what he'd been missing. Slowly, wordlessly, he sat up, pulled her up beside him, then tipped her chin up, closed his eyes, and melted into her.

The moment their lips met, it was as if he'd been waiting forever to hold her in his arms, and he drank her in hungrily, urgently, needing the contact, the pressure of her arms around him, her lips on his, their bodies entwined. He didn't need Beth, he thought angrily. And he would prove it.

Time stretched—and it felt like they'd been on the rock, folded into each others' arms, forever, would be forever—

And then Harper pushed him away.

"I can't, Adam," she whispered.

"Harper—" He reached out for her.

"No, not like this," she protested, sitting up and drawing away from him.

"Is it too fast? Is it—"

"It's too soon, Adam," she said tenderly. "You're hurt. You're angry." She brushed his hair out of his face and kissed him on the cheek. "When we do this . . . *if* we do this . . . I don't want it to be because you want to get revenge on Beth."

"I'd never *use* you, Harper," he protested.

"I know that—don't you think I know that? But I think . . . I think we should wait. Until you know what you really want."

I want you. That's what he wanted to say. But the words choked in his throat because he knew she was right. And she didn't deserve that. He didn't deserve that.

He lay back on the rock again, sighing.

"I'm so fucked up, Harper," he admitted. "How did things get so fucked up? I don't know what I'm supposed to do now. I just don't know."

She kissed him softly on the lips and then lay back beside him, taking his hand.

"We'll figure it out, Adam. Together."

The night had seemed interminable. Harper had disappeared into the woods, and Greg had refused to listen to her apology, so Miranda had picked her way through the forest, following the narrow path back toward Valley Glen High School. Alone. She'd made her way to the parking lot and stood by the empty Haven bus. Alone.

Finally, the pizza party had ended, the Haven High fans had surged into the parking lot and boarded their bus and the van, and now Miranda was speeding toward home. And, slouched down in a seat right behind the driver, peering out the window into the darkness, she was still alone. Completely and utterly alone.

She hadn't noticed whether Harper, Adam, and Greg had made it back in time, and she didn't really care. It's not like any of them were worried about her, wondering where she was or if she was all right. Harper's amazing disappearing act had made that pretty clear.

No, she was on her own—and maybe, she thought bitterly, she'd better get used to it. After all, who understood her? Who was there for her when *she* needed someone to lean on? Good old Miranda, always there to lend a sympathetic ear, always ready to give advice—but when was it ever *her* turn? When she was the one who needed help, who needed some support, then there she was—alone.

What was the point of putting everything you had into a friendship when all you got back was . . . well, nothing?

She leaned back against the worn leather of the bus seat, trying to get comfortable, trying to ignore the shouts and laughter coming from the seats behind her. She closed her eyes, willing herself to be tired, to lose herself in sleep. But her mind refused to relax.

It was a five-hour ride back home, and she had nothing to do but curl up in the dark, wide awake, and contemplate the misery of her own existence.

Good thing she had enough material to last her the rest of the night.

They rode home on the van together, side by side, hand in hand. Adam had decided he was in no shape to ride on the rowdier fan bus with most of the team. As the van pulled onto the road, he wrapped an arm around Harper, pulling her close, then closed his eyes and leaned his head back against the seat. She snuggled up against him, her head on his chest, and listened to his heart, beating in time with the gentle rocking of the van.

She felt so warm, so safe with him by her side. And the taste of him was still on her lips—she'd waited so long for him to look at her like that, to hold her like that. Which had made it all the harder to push him away. Even harder than it had been to watch him in all that pain, to watch him raging against himself and the world and know that she could end it for him with just a few quick words—but that doing so would cost her everything. So she'd stayed silent, played the loyal and dutiful friend—and it had worked. Better, and faster, than she'd ever imagined.

It didn't matter how she'd gotten here, she reasoned. All that mattered was that she was here now, and she was close, so painfully close, to getting everything she wanted. She just had to be careful—she couldn't rush it, couldn't let him rush it. Patience, time—and then, the big payoff.

As the night wore on, a deep quiet settled over them. Harper closed her eyes and breathed in Adam's closeness; in the quiet dark, it felt like they were all alone in the world. Together. She leaned against him, her cheek resting on his chest, rising and falling with his steady breaths, slowly drifting off to sleep. After so much time and energy spent planning the next step, looking toward tomorrow, and the day after that, Harper had finally found herself in a moment she could enjoy for what it was, a moment she wished would last forever.

If only it could.

chapter

13

Adam awoke the next morning with a sick feeling in the pit of his stomach. It was as if, even before he was fully awake, even before his mind had wrapped itself around the horror of the night before, his body had known that something was deeply, deeply wrong. When he'd staggered home last night at three a.m., a part of him had wanted to call Beth, to drive over to her house, bang on the windows until she let him in, shake her until she admitted what she'd done.

He'd wanted to call her last night, the moment he'd found out. But he'd stopped himself. It wasn't because he was afraid he'd say something he shouldn't—it was because he wanted to see her face, wanted her to be there right in front of him when he told her exactly what he thought of her. He didn't want anything—not static, not some misplaced twinge of pity or forgiveness—to get in the way.

He knew that this moment, coming face-to-face with

her, would be the hardest one to get through, that if he were going to crack, were going to buy the inevitable denial and tearful "have pity on me" routine, it would be then. But he also knew that if he could get through the encounter without breaking, he could be rid of her forever.

It was Harper who'd convinced him, who'd persuaded him to wait until he'd calmed down and his head was clear—or at least until morning. And now morning was here. A storm of anger was still simmering just beneath the surface—he was almost afraid to pick up the phone. Once he released himself, once he let out all the emotion he'd been bottling up since the night before—he didn't know how he'd stand it.

But he couldn't do nothing. That would be worse.

So Adam rolled out of bed and dialed the familiar number, suppressing his nausea and affecting a cheerful, innocent voice.

"I'm so happy you called!" she said.

"I missed you!" she said.

"I can't believe you won!" she said.

Adam choked out a few terse sentences. He was fine. He was tired. He wanted to see her.

"I want to see you, too!" she gushed. "I'm stuck at work all day, but tonight we're going to Bourquin's, for some last-minute studying. Meet me there?"

We?

Perfect.

Beth shifted her weight back and forth outside the coffee shop, then began to pace along the front of the restaurant.

Kane waved at her through the glass window, and she gave him a weak smile.

She couldn't wait for Adam to arrive. These last few days had been so confusing—her and Adam not speaking, Kane always underfoot, and then last night, in the park . . .

She just needed to see Adam again, soon, to talk to him, touch him, remind herself that he was real, that *he* was her life, that everything else was just—just misplaced emotion. She'd been stressed, things had been weird between them for so long, but now it could all be over. The SATs were tomorrow morning, and after that, she promised herself, she'd stop. Take a break from overachieving, just for a little while, take a break from the dutiful daughter routine, change her shifts around at the restaurant. She'd even promise not to see Kane again, if that's what it took. She and Adam would have the chance, finally, to be together, to heal. One more night, and she'd be all his—she couldn't wait to tell him.

Adam had spent the day cleaning out the garage, hoping to keep his mind off things. It was all he could do to keep from running down to the diner and confronting Beth— but he'd decided it would be better to wait. That night, she and Kane would be together. Which meant he could kill two birds with one very large stone.

For hours upon hours he had sorted through the junk in the garage, boxing up most of it to be taken down to the town dump. Just before taping up the last box, he'd slipped his new trophy inside, then closed the lid again. He didn't need a reminder of the day before sitting on his shelf, mocking him. He didn't need to remember how happy he'd been, how good he'd felt about himself and his life, before everything came crashing down. The trophy was nothing but garbage now—just like his relationship.

As the sun set Adam walked over to the coffee shop— it was a long way, but then, he had a lot of energy to burn. He saw her before she saw him. She stood just under the neon sign, her features lit softly by the bluish glow. Angelic, he might have thought, in a different life. She looked at her watch and began pacing. She was waiting for him—or maybe she was wondering how much time she'd have to waste on him before getting back to her secret lover.

Bile rose within him, and for a moment he thought he might be sick. But then he forced away the image of her and Kane (when he closed his eyes, he imagined them screwing everywhere—on her bed, in his car, in the locker room, on the basketball court—her poison had tainted everything and everywhere in his life). He needed to be calm. Strong.

Things were going to get worse before they got better.

"Adam!" she called, as soon as she spotted him approaching. "I'm so glad to see you—I missed you!" She ran over to give him a hug, but when she tried to kiss him, he turned his face away.

"Are you still mad?" It seemed an unnecessary question. She'd been hoping that a couple days away had made him realize he had nothing to worry about, that she and Kane were just friends. And that was it, she thought, pushing away the memory of last night. That was it.

"Now, why would I be mad?" his voice sounded strange. Hard. "Did you and Kane have a good time without me?"

"It was horrible," she lied. "All we did was study. I'm so burnt out—I just need to get some sleep."

"Yeah, I bet you do. I bet you're *real* tired."

"What?" What was he getting at?

"Just drop it, Beth," he said harshly.

"What?"

"The innocent act. The little miss perfect shit. It's tired, and I'm not buying it anymore."

"What act? Why are you being like this?" She reached out a hand to him, but he shrugged it off, jerking away as if her touch burned.

"Don't touch me," he said sharply.

Beth took a step back. Her heart was thumping in her ears, and a sense of dread had settled over her.

"Adam, what's going on?"

"I guess you thought I'd never figure it out."

"Figure what out?" she asked.

"You must think I'm an idiot or something."

"Of course I don't—what are you—?"

"Just shut up already!" he roared. "I can't stand it anymore. Stop looking at me like you give a shit, stop acting like you're all confused, all pure and sweet and innocent— I know all about it, all about you and . . . him."

He jerked his thumb toward the window of the coffee shop—Kane was inside, looking out with obvious concern.

"This again?" Beth asked, tears welling up at the corners of her eyes. "I told you, there's nothing going on."

"And I told *you*—I know everything. Kaia *saw* you, Beth. I guess you thought you'd be safe, but she saw you. And she told me everything."

Beth's mind skidded across the last forty-eight hours—
what could Kaia have seen? What could she have said to
make him this angry? The night in the park, it had just
been innocent. It might have looked . . . but it had been
innocent. Completely. And besides—*Kaia*?

"Kaia? You're yelling at me because of something *Kaia*
told you?" Beth asked incredulously. "Kaia's a liar and a
bitch, Adam, you're the one who told me that. Why would
you believe anything she has to say? Why would you
believe her over me?"

"Oh, *Kaia's* a liar? *Kaia's* a bitch?" He forced a laugh.
"That's a good one, Beth. You know, I didn't believe her
either, not at first. I defended you—I defended your *honor*."
He laughed again, bitterly. "Good thing for her, she had *pictures*."

Pictures? Beth's heart leaped into her throat. What
could there even be pictures of? They hadn't even kissed.
There had been one moment when—but no. Whatever she
may have imagined doing, *nothing* had happened. Nothing.

"Adam, nothing happened," she protested. "You've got
to believe me. This is just a huge misunderstanding. If
you'll just listen to me—"

"I'm done listening to you," he snapped. "I'm done
with your lies. Do you have any idea what it felt like? To
see you with him? I should have turned last night with
Harper into a Kodak moment for you, then maybe you
could see how it feels."

Beth, who already felt as if she'd been punched in the
stomach, staggered back and had to lean against the wall for
support.

"Harper? You and Harper?"

He looked surprised for a moment, as if not realizing he'd said it aloud. Then his face twisted into an ugly smile.

"That's right, Harper. But why should you even care? I hope to hell you do." He glared at her, and she couldn't bring herself to look away. "I hope it hurts."

It was as if Adam had disappeared into the desert, and some heartless, unfeeling monster had returned in his place. Beth was reeling.

"So, what—you get a phone call or something from *Kaia*, of all people, and then without even bothering to talk to me, you just jump into bed with someone else? What's wrong with you?" she cried.

"You are *not* the victim here," he spat. "So you can just knock off the tears. It's not going to work."

She lunged forward and grabbed both of his hands tightly in hers. If she could just make him stop for a minute. Think. Before throwing everything away.

"Adam, just wait—can we just—"

"Enough!" He shoved her backward, and she stumbled back against the wall. "Don't touch me again, Beth. I mean it."

That was when she knew. It was over. This person, this thing in front of her who spit out all this hate and anger and venom, who took Kaia's word over hers, who let Harper—

She couldn't even think about it. Couldn't even look at him.

"Just go, then, Adam," she said wearily through her tears. "If that's how you feel, why don't you just go?"

"One more piece of unfinished business," Adam replied, looking over her shoulder. She turned—Kane stood in the doorway.

"Everything okay out here?" he asked with concern.

"Hey, bro, everything's just fine. Why don't you come on out for a little talk?" Adam said heartily.

Kane looked back and forth between the two of them.

"It doesn't *look* fine," he said hesitantly, walking toward Beth, who was now slumped against the wall, her head in her hands. He put a hand on her shoulder. "Beth, are you—"

"Don't touch her," Adam snapped, knocking Kane's arm away roughly.

"What's your problem?" Kane asked, turning to face him.

"You were," Adam said. Suddenly, he punched Kane in the face, hard, knocking him to the ground. "But not anymore."

As Kane moaned in pain and Beth looked on in horror, Adam slowly turned his back on them and walked away.

"She's all yours now," he called over his shoulder. "You two deserve each other."

Kane lay on the ground for a moment, moaning—with a few small whimpers thrown in, just for effect. (Not too many, though—it wouldn't do to have her thinking he was some kind of wimp.) Then he slowly pulled himself up and walked over to Beth, who was frozen in place, staring after Adam's disappearing figure.

Kane said a silent congratulations to Kaia and Harper—apparently, everything had gone like clockwork. His turn now.

He put a comforting arm around Beth, trying to still her heaving sobs.

She leaned against him for a moment, burying her face

in his chest and crying. *It's going to be a bitch to get all of that snot out of the fabric,* he thought. *But after all this hard work, what's a little more?* So he held her, wishing his hands could stray downward, but he held back, just rubbing her shoulder blades and making comforting noises. Patience, he counseled himself.

"Beth, maybe you want to go inside and talk?" he finally suggested.

At the sound of his voice, she looked up in alarm, almost as if she'd forgotten he was there. She twisted away from him.

"I—I have to go," she said, wild eyed, backing away from the restaurant.

"Okay," he said quietly, trying to calm her down. It unsettled him, somehow, to see her like this. It wasn't that he felt guilty, he insisted to himself. Or that he couldn't stand to see her hurt. It was just—unsettling. Guys and crying don't mix, he decided. That was all. "Let me get my keys. I'll drive you home," he offered.

"No—no!" she yelped. "I just need to be by myself. I just need to go."

"Beth, I'm not letting you wander out there by yourself," he said in alarm. "Not when you're . . . like this."

But it was too late—she'd run off into the darkness.

Once she was safely gone, he shook his head and shrugged. So he'd have to wait. Another day, maybe two. Not a problem. He could be patient. Now that everything was in place, there was nothing standing in his way, he just had to wait.

She'd come back.

They always did.

✧✧✧

Harper was antsy. She knew she should study—she might not care about the SATs, but it couldn't hurt to spend a couple hours at least *looking* at her books, just so she could say she'd done something.

But she was too excited to concentrate. She couldn't just sit there and study, not while she was stuck in this weird limbo between triumph and actually reaping the benefits of her victory. She couldn't sit still, couldn't stay inside—she wanted to dance, to leap, to drink, to show the world that she was the girl who had everything.

She wanted, in essence, to go out.

Adam was off somewhere with Beth, breaking her heart, she hoped.

Kane, if he was smart, was lurking about, ready to pick up the pieces.

Miranda, she was pretty sure, wasn't speaking to her. A problem for another day.

She supposed she could call up some of the girls, just choose some names at random from her cell and sucker them into going out—but she didn't want that. She didn't want to have to make up an excuse, to have to pretend that today was just another day when in fact today was *the* day, the start of everything, the day the world was about to open up for her. She wanted someone who would celebrate with her—and know what she was celebrating.

With surprise, she realized what it was—she wanted Kaia.

As she whirled under the lights of Grace's only "dance club"—a large and half empty bar that played cheesy eighties hits on Friday nights, Kaia was surprised to discover that she was actually having something akin to a good time.

Jack Powell was in for the night. Friday nights were his, and his alone, he'd informed her, and she'd figured that meant she'd be spending a quiet night at home watching TV and painting her nails. (Let these small-town losers study for the SATs—she'd aced the test last spring with the help of Ivy Bound, an intense one-on-one prep program for mediocre rich kids. So Kaia couldn't care less what happened in the morning.) And then Harper had called, and here they were, downing poorly mixed Cosmos and flailing their arms around to old-school Madonna—two material girls out on the town. For what it was.

And why not? Hadn't they triumphed over the forces of good and managed to win the fair-haired couple over to the dark side? Harper looked happier than Kaia had ever seen her, and Kaia knew it was more than the vodka.

So let her be happy, Kaia thought. She doesn't deserve it, but then, who the hell does? Why not Harper? Why not all of them?

Harper swung her arms around Kaia and they belted out the lyrics of the chorus together, at the top of their lungs.

"Don't get any ideas," Harper shouted, trying to make herself heard over the music. "I still can't stand you!"

"Don't worry, the feeling is mutual," Kaia yelled, grinning. She spun around and raised her arms above her head, twisting and turning to the steady beat.

It was a scene Kaia would have been hideously embarrassed to witness back in New York, much less participate in—the only people who danced to eighties music were bridge and tunnel chicks trolling for men in the big city, and men with gold teeth and bad breath looking for their next lay.

No, the number one rule of her life in the Big Apple: Only losers look like they're having fun. Boredom is the new chic.

But here? There was no one to see her—no one who counted, at least. There was only her, Harper, the flashing lights, the drinks, the steady beat and the vibrating floor. She closed her eyes and let the music fill her up, sweeping over her and carrying her body away.

Adam had left a sweatshirt in her room the last time he was there. The last time—maybe it was just that, the last time he would ever be there. Beth moaned and curled up into a tight ball, burying her face in the soft cotton of the shirt. It still smelled like him.

She closed her bloodshot eyes and breathed in deeply, letting herself pretend, for a moment, that he was in the room, lying down beside her, his arms around her, that she was safe.

But it was no use. Her bed was empty—and a sweatshirt, a scent, a thinning memory, was all she had left.

It came in waves: the sadness, the terrifying feeling of being completely alone, completely out of control. It came in waves—she'd heard the phrase before, but never really understood what it meant. That when they came, the powerful feelings swept over her, knocking her down and tossing her about as if she'd been caught by the blast of a wall of water. It lifted her off her feet, spun her, slammed her into the ground, and dragged her, tired and teary and confused, to shore, to safety, to the relative peace that would rule until another wave swept in and knocked her down all over again.

There were moments, brief moments, where she thought she would be okay, that all the pain and sorrow sweeping over her would end, that it would drag her down, but not forever. And then there were other moments, long, interminable moments, when she feared she would drown.

He was drowning—in anger, in despair, in indecision, in regret.

Had he done the right thing?

Was he a complete hypocrite? Sleeping with someone else and then dumping on Beth for doing the same? Had he made a horrible mistake?

Adam sat on the floor of his bedroom, door shut tight, loud music drowning out the rest of the world—if only it could drown out his thoughts. But they were too loud.

In front of him sat a pile of pictures, pictures that Beth had given him over the past couple years, pictures of the two of them together, happy.

There they were in the mountains, and there, in another, curled up together on the couch. Beth, cheering in the stands at one of his basketball games. Beth, cheeks flushed, eyes radiant, balanced on her toes to give him a kiss on the cheek. Beth, elegant and lovely, in her silver evening gown at last year's spring formal.

He held the last picture in his hands—it had always been his favorite and, until this evening, had sat on his desk in a silver frame. It had been taken just after they'd started going out. They were in the park. It had been a rare, beautiful day—cool air, brilliant blue sky. Even the grass had seemed lush and green. Adam had swept Beth up in his arms, dangling her above the ground, and she was laughing, trying unsuccessfully to get away, her hair billowing in the wind, her face filled with joy—his face filled with love. It was how he always thought of her—open, happy, laughing, so in love with him, so hopeful about the future. She'd believed in them—believed in him.

He held the picture, wondering: Had he made a mistake? Thrown away something too precious, too perfect to lose?

But then he remembered that these weren't the only pictures, that these images no longer told the whole story. He looked out the window, to Harper's dark bedroom only a few feet away, and remembered who he could count on—and who he couldn't, who had taken everything good in his life, everything he'd thought was real, and stomped on it. Destroyed it.

This picture in front of him that he'd loved so much— it was a lie. Everything he'd loved had been a lie.

He tore the picture in half, right down the middle, and threw it aside.

He was done with lies, forever.

chapter

14

The next morning Harper ran out the door at eight a.m. sharp to meet Adam, who was driving her to school for the dreaded test. She was still hungover from the night before, and she expected he'd look even worse, but instead, Adam was clean shaven and bright-eyed, and had a wide smile on his face. Too wide, Harper decided, but if he wanted to pretend nothing had happened, she'd respect that and go along with it. For a while.

"Excuse me while I have a heart attack," he joked when she climbed into the car. "Harper Grace? *On time?* Will wonders never cease?"

"Hold the applause and let's get going," she sighed, squinting in the bright morning sun. "The sooner we get started, the sooner we can get this thing over with."

"Amen to that," he agreed, and shifted the car into gear.

The whole ride was like that—pleasant small talk, strange and unnerving only because it was so utterly and completely normal. As they pulled into the lot, they passed right by Beth's car, but Adam said nothing—maybe he hadn't noticed.

The car pulled to a stop, and they got out. Harper took a deep breath. "Well, should we go face our future?"

She began to walk toward the school, but Adam grabbed her hand and pulled her back to the car.

"Wait," he said, smiling. "I have a present for you."

He pulled a small, hastily wrapped package from his pocket and handed it to her. She ripped off the wrapping.

"A new cell phone?" she asked, surprised.

"To replace the one I broke," he explained, blushing. "Sorry, again."

"Oh, Adam, you know, I don't care about the phone," she assured him. "I mean, thank you—this is so sweet, but—how are *you* doing?"

He shrugged and looked away. "Okay, I guess."

She took a step closer to him and put her hands on his shoulders, forcing him to look her in the eye. "How are you *really* doing?"

Slowly, carefully, as if afraid it might hurt, he smiled. A real smile, this time.

"I think I'm really okay," he told her. "Now."

And he leaned toward her, and they kissed, and it was sweet and soft and perfect—and again, she forced herself to push him away.

"Adam, I told you—," she protested.

He wrapped his arms around her waist and pulled her close to him, bending his lips to her ear, and whispered the words she'd been waiting so long to hear.

"I don't want revenge," he promised. "I want *you.*"

❖❖❖

She didn't think it would hit her so hard.

One minute, Beth was on her feet, barely awake, barely functional, but still upright, moving forward.

And the next, there they were, Adam and Harper, locked in each other's arms.

It was as if all the breath was sucked from her lungs, all the energy leeched from her body. The world narrowed to a pinhole vision—all she could see was him, with her, those familiar hands all over another body. She knew every inch of him, could almost feel what he was feeling as Harper wrapped herself around him. She wanted to throw up— instead she staggered, would have collapsed, but a pair of strong arms caught her halfway to the ground.

Kane.

"Beth, you look terrible," he said, helping her up and putting his arm around her. She leaned against him grate-fully.

"Thanks," she said weakly as they shuffled toward the school. "A girl always likes to hear that." She did look ter-rible, she knew that. She'd cried all night, and it showed. When she'd looked in the mirror this morning, she had barely recognized the pale, gaunt face looking back at her with dead, hopeless eyes. "You don't look so great your-self," she added, gesturing toward the angry, enflamed skin around his left eye.

"You should see the other guy," Kane joked—then looked appalled, as he realized what he had said. "Beth, I'm sorry, I didn't mean—"

"It's okay." But it wasn't. It might never be.

"Beth, I want you to know, if you need—"

She put up a hand to silence him.

"Can we not do this now? I just need to—I just need to make it through the test."

It was as far ahead as she could bear to look. The future, which started in three hours, would take care of itself.

Three hours.

One hundred eighty minutes.

Too many questions to count—and a whole future riding on every answer.

Miranda bit nervously on the eraser of her number two pencil. Maybe she should have spent a little more time studying and a little less time partying. Too late now.

Kane tapped his toes, checked his watch, and waited for the time to run out. After all that time pretending to be an idiot, it was almost a pleasure to run through the test, fill in all the answers with ease, and kick back and relax. But he wished the clock hand would move just a little faster. He had things to do.

Kaia filled in the bubbles at random, making pictures with the dots and trying to spell out as many words as she could with the letters *A*, *B*, *C*, *D*, and *E*. Who knew, maybe she'd score even better this time. If so, she could patent the method and drive the Ivy Bound assholes out of business.

Harper fidgeted. This sucked. Stuck inside, alone, trapped behind a desk, when Adam sat somewhere behind her. Was he watching her? she wondered. Did he finally want her as much as she wanted him? As soon as this thing was done, they were heading home—her parents were out for the day, and she and Adam had a *lot* of catching up to do. Now it was just a matter of running down the clock.

Adam didn't want to be there. The test didn't mean anything to him—he wasn't going anywhere, test or no test. He knew that. So why waste his time? He watched Beth, a few rows in front of him, her blond head bent intently over the page. *I hope it was worth it to you,* he thought bitterly. It had all started with this stupid test. *I sure as hell hope it was worth it.*

The numbers and words swam in front of her, blurred by tears. Beth's mind was fuzzy with fatigue, and it was all she could do to keep her heavy lids from slipping shut. To sleep would be such bliss—to forget all of this, to forget about him, a few rows back. Was he looking at her? Or was he looking at Harper? She didn't even know how many sections she'd already finished, only knew that the test had dragged on forever—and that her answer sheet was still almost completely blank.

She'd heard that you got six hundred points just for filling in your name. . . . She was going to need it.

Free at last, Miranda thought, stepping out of the stuffy school and breathing a relieved breath of warm, fresh air. But her celebration was short-lived, for what good was celebrating when you were all alone?

Harper, who she still wasn't speaking to, was a few steps ahead. When they hit the parking lot, Adam ran up to her and swept her off her feet with a hug and a passionate kiss.

Big surprise, Miranda thought. *Harper gets everything she wants. Again.*

And there, only a few feet away, were Beth and—of all people—Kane. On another day Miranda might have been heartbroken—but today? Today she just accepted the new development and moved on. She was in the kind of mood where the worst case scenario seemed pretty much the only option—which meant she wasn't much surprised when it happened.

Beth looked like she'd been hit by a train (small wonder, considering the way her boyfriend, or maybe ex-boyfriend, Miranda supposed, was all over Harper). But it looked like Kane was disgustingly determined to cheer her up.

No, Miranda wouldn't waste her time worrying about Beth. Or any of them. Why should she? They all had some-one—and then there was her. As always.

Alone.

Beth had pushed Kane away, and, thinking she wanted to be alone, needed to be alone, she'd driven over to the old elementary school playground, her place, the place that always felt like home.

But as soon as she stepped through the opening in the chain link fence, she knew she'd made a mistake.

Beth had thought she would want to be there. She thought it would remind her of life beyond Adam, of childhood, of happiness. But the past suddenly seemed bleak—because all that hope had led her here, to the empty present. The playground didn't wrap her in the soft arms of memory. It didn't fix anything. It was just a cold, strange place, made all the stranger by the fact that it was so famil-iar, that it was completely unchanged.

She was the one who'd changed.

She walked over to the swings, always her favorite spot, and sat down on one, pushing herself back and forth. Even the swings felt wrong, off. The seat was too tight, her legs were too long, scraping the ground. She was too old, and her body no longer remembered what to do, how to be that child who swung so high, pumping her legs, scraping the sky. *That's what happens when you get older,* she realized. You feel a little sick as the swing sways back and forth, but not enough to stop, and only at one point, when you've gone as far back and as high up as you can, and you're almost parallel with the ground, you stop in midair, then lurch back into motion a moment before your stomach does, swooping toward the ground. You wonder whether your swing could flip over the metal bar at the top, swing you all the way around, and throw you to the ground, bruised and broken. When you were a kid, you thought it could happen—but you weren't afraid. All grown up, you know it can't happen—but you're filled with fear. You swing slower, instead of pumping for the sky. You don't jump off—you slow yourself to a stop. You'd never fling yourself into the air in midswing, because you're no longer dreaming of flying. You're just worrying about how you're going to land.

This is what it means to get old, Beth thought. *To grow up. To be alone.*

It sucked.

"I thought I'd find you here."

It was Kane, appearing in front of her as if from nowhere. He always appeared just when she most needed someone, as if he somehow knew.

He sat down on the swing next to her.

"Should I ask how the test went?" he asked hesitantly.

She didn't know if it was the reminder of the bombed SATs or just the warmth and concern in his voice, but she burst into tears.

"I'll take that as a no," he said, and scooped her into his arms. And this time she let him hold her, let him comfort her, melted into his warm, strong body, let herself be supported by someone else—because she could no longer do it herself.

He rubbed her back, gently kissed the top of her head, and then—and she knew it was coming, hadn't she always known it was coming?—he tilted her face toward him and kissed her.

She was about to pull away. But then she thought of Adam and Harper, of facing another moment on her own all by herself, of drowning.

She was so tired, too tired to think, too tired to resist.

She pulled back for a moment and looked into his eyes. They were warm and caring. She took a deep breath, and kissed him—and let herself go.

What did she have left to lose?

Kaia stood by the fence at the end of the playground, watching and smiling.

Happily ever after, she thought—or, at least, happy for another couple weeks until the whole mess blows up in their faces.

She looked again at Kane and Beth, one of the more mismatched twosomes she'd ever seen. All four of them were flirting with disaster, and Kaia was more than happy to help things along. It passed the time, after all.

Besides, she was good at it—making trouble, causing chaos. She may not know how to make herself happy—but she was damn good at making other people miserable.

And she was just getting started.

Here's a taste of the next *sinful* read . . .

Pride

Kaia pulled her car into the lot of the Lost and Found and switched off the ignition, slamming a fist into the steering wheel.

She didn't know *why* she was so angry. It's not like she and Jack Powell were "going steady" or something pathetically absurd like that. You couldn't cheat on someone if you weren't in a relationship, right? Yes, he'd forbidden her to see other guys, and she'd accepted it, for the sake of keeping their secret. He was right, high school boys *did* get jealous—and eventually curious. But, she realized, *he'd* never promised not to see other women. And she had never thought to ask.

And why would she? Wasn't that their thing? No obligations, no attachments, no messy emotions screwing things up and getting in the way.

So she had no right to be mad, no right to be jealous. And if her ego had taken a hit, realizing that apparently she wasn't enough for him—well, her ego was pretty tough. It would survive.

He'd wanted her to pity him, stuck in the mountains on some ski trip with a bunch of high schoolers.

"I'd so much rather be with you," he'd sworn.

Right. Me—or the first blond who crosses his path. Same difference.

She picked up the flyer she'd tossed on the passenger seat: BLIND MONKEYS! ONE NIGHT ONLY AT THE LOST AND FOUND!

Reed was the lead singer and had told her about the concert—and of course she'd immediately blown him off. Garage bands, dive bars, and Kaia didn't mix.

But tonight, after Harper's call, she'd suddenly changed her tune.

Not that she had a sudden craving for smoky air and off-key covers—and certainly she had no particular interest in seeing Reed Sawyer again. She wouldn't go out of her way for someone like him.

Nor was she willing to admit that the thought of Powell with another girl—another woman—had driven her so crazy with jealousy that she'd hopped in the car and driven to this dead end pit of a bar to throw herself at a pizza-boy-cum-tow-truck-driver-cum-high-school-dropout-to-be.

So what the hell am I doing here? she thought irritably. *I should just turn around and go.* Now.

But instead she opened the door, got out of the BMW, and headed toward the bar.

She didn't know why she was there or what she was getting herself into—but there was only one way to find out.

✧✧✧

"Oh, that feels *so* good," Kane moaned. He leaned his head back against the rim of the hot tub and closed his eyes. "I could stay here forever."

"Mmm, I know what you mean." Beth stretched out along her side, reveling in the jets of hot water pummeling her sore muscles. Her face tingled in the cold night air.

It was an almost perfect end to an almost perfect day.

Kane hadn't asked anything about her afternoon, and she wasn't about to volunteer the fact that she'd spent the whole time with Adam, skiing and laughing—and loving every minute of it. It had felt almost like old times, the two of them together, anticipating each other's every move, the easy ebb and flow of conversation. As if he'd let himself forget everything that had happened—at least until the end of the day, when they'd parted. They had stayed on safe topics all afternoon, meaningless chatter about the ski trip, about college applications—but in the end, it had seemed as if he were finally about to say something that mattered. Then he'd spotted Kane in the distance—and his whole face had frozen. That was it. He'd waved a brusque good-bye and walked off toward the lodge, as if the whole day had never happened. And they were right back where they'd started.

But it's a beginning, Beth thought hopefully. *And maybe now we can—*

She cut herself off. Can what? Get back together? It's not like she was still in love with him, or even wanted him back. *Friendship,* she assured herself. That's all she wanted. To reach a point where they wouldn't have to ignore each other in the halls. To know something about what was going on in his life. To have him care what was going on in hers.

That was it—nothing more.

She was with Kane now, right where she wanted to be.

He floated lazily across the hot tub to join her on her side and playfully flicked some of the churning water in her face.

She giggled—but before she could splash him back, he grabbed her hands and kissed her.

"You look pretty spectacular in a bikini," he commented when they broke for air, giving her an appreciative glance. "Anyone ever told you that?"

Beth blushed and sank a bit deeper into the water, suddenly very aware of how much of her was exposed.

When she didn't reply, he grinned and flexed a bicep. "Traditionally, now's the time when you tell me how handsome and sexy I look," he pointed out.

Now she splashed him. "Yes, you're a total hottie, babe," she gushed in her best Barbie voice.

He leaned back and closed his eyes again, his face plastered with a smug smile. "Mock me all you want—but you know you wish I were wearing a Speedo."

Beth laughed and nestled herself against him, relaxing into the delicious warmth of the water, the brittle sting of the winter air, the solid body beside her. She suddenly felt very tired—and very content.

So tired and so content that she let her guard down for a moment—and the question she'd been holding in for so long just slipped out.

"Kane?"

"Mmm?"

"Why are you with me?"

He began idly rubbing his hand up and down her arm.

"I thought we just established that," he said lightly, without opening his eyes. "You're one hot babe, I'm one hot babe—makes perfect sense to me."

"Seriously, Kane—we've got nothing in common."

"We both like hot tubs," he pointed out. "And bikinis . . ."

She rolled her eyes.

"Come on," she said, exasperated. "I mean it. We're totally different—and I'm nothing like any of the girls you dated before."

He opened his eyes then and sat up and took her hand.

"Have I ever made you think that's a bad thing?" he asked gently.

"No, I just—"

"You're right—you're nothing like them, Beth. And *that's* why I'm with you."

"I just think people must look at us and wonder," Beth sighed. "We don't seem to make any sense." She didn't know why she was saying all these things, not now, but it was as if once she'd started, she couldn't stop herself. She'd been holding it all in for so long.

"We make sense to *me*," he insisted. "Who cares what other people think? They don't know us—they don't know me."

Beth touched her hand to his cheek. "Sometimes . . ." She paused—but she'd come so far already, why stop? "Sometimes, I feel like *I* don't know you."

She could feel him tense beneath her fingers, and he shifted away.

"You know me," he countered. "This is me—what you see is what you get. I'm easy."

Beth shook her head. "That's got to be the biggest lie

you've ever told me. Easy?" She smiled fondly. "Not so much."

"What do you want from me?" he asked petulantly.

Beth draped an arm around him, wishing he hadn't gotten so defensive—she didn't want to fight. She just wanted to talk. They never did much of that, she realized.

"I guess I just want . . . more," she told him honestly. Spending time with Adam today had reminded her of what it was like to *really* know someone—and she wanted that again, somehow. "I really like you, Kane, and I just want more of you—I want to know all of you."

He perked up suddenly.

"Something else we have in common," he pointed out. "I want to know all of you, too. Your lips," he kissed her gently. "Your neck." He kissed her again, soft, brief kisses that grazed her chin and ran down the length of her long neck. "Your beautiful—"

"Kane!" she squirmed away. "We're in public!"

"You're right," he replied, gaping at the surroundings as if he'd only just noticed. "What are we doing here? Come on." He stood and extended a hand to her. "Let's go back to my room—we can start this whole getting to know each other thing."

She stood—without his help—and grabbed a towel as she stepped out of the hot tub and onto the steamy patio. "That's not what I mean, and you know it."

"Hey, get your mind out of the gutter. I meant we should go back to my room and talk . . . for a while." He draped another towel around her shoulders and pulled her close to him, rubbing her shivering body to warm her up. "I really like you, too, Beth," he whispered in her ear. "You're not the only one who wants more."

Beth took a deep breath and closed her eyes, resting her head against his dripping chest. Part of her wanted to go with him—*all* of her wanted to go with him, in fact. Why not? He was handsome and charming, his smile made her tremble, they were in this beautiful, romantic resort, and for whatever reason, he wanted to be with her. And, she realized, she wanted to be with him.

So what was the problem? Why did the thought of stepping into his room and closing the door behind her make her heart race and her muscles tense? She knew what he was expecting out of this weekend—had every right to expect, she supposed. She'd known it from the start. So why did the thought make her hyperventilate?

What is wrong *with me?* She thought in frustration. She'd let her fears torpedo her relationship with Adam—was she going to be alone the rest of her life because of her stupid issues? Kane wasn't Adam—he'd been patient with her so far, but patience wasn't in his nature, she could tell. How long would he wait?

She opened her mouth to tell him, "Yes, let's go back to your room"—but couldn't choke out the words.

"I've got to go back to my room and dry off, take a shower," she said lamely. She gave him a long kiss, then extricated herself from his embrace.

"You can shower in my—"

"I'll come over later, when I'm done," she promised.

And she so wanted it to be the truth.

But she knew herself.

And so she knew better.

about the author

Robin Wasserman enjoys writing about high school—but wakes up every day grateful that she doesn't have to relive it. She recently abandoned the beaches and boulevards of Los Angeles for the chilly embrace of the East Coast, as all that sun and fun gave her too little to complain about. She now lives and writes in New York City, which she claims to love for its vibrant culture and intellectual life. In reality, she doesn't make it to museums nearly enough, and actually just loves the city for its pizza, its shopping, and the fact that at 3 a.m. you can always get anything you need—and you can get it delivered.

FEARLESS FBI

Special Agent, Gaia Moore

In a sophisticated new twist on Francine Pascal's bestselling Fearless series, Gaia's out of college and training for the FBI. Solving real cases, tracking real criminals . . . it takes strength, intelligence, and fierce determination.

But while the FBI has strict codes and procedures, Gaia has never been a team player.

And when it comes to hunting down a serial killer, cracking the case may mean bending FBI rules. For Gaia, it means breaking them.

#1 KILL GAME

#2 LIVE BAIT

#3 AGENT OUT

By Francine Pascal

From Simon Pulse • Published by Simon & Schuster

Sharper. Older. More dangerous than ever.

UGLIES
SCOTT WESTERFELD

Everybody gets to be supermodel gorgeous. What could be wrong with that?

In this futuristic world, all children are born "uglies," or freaks. But on their sixteenth birthdays they are given extreme makeovers and turned "pretty." Then their whole lives change. . . .

PRAISE FOR *UGLIES*:

★ "An exciting series. . . . The awesome ending thrills with potential." *—Kirkus Reviews*

★ "Ingenious . . . high-concept YA fiction that has wide appeal." *—Booklist*

★ "Highly readable with a convincing plot that incorporates futuristic technologies and a disturbing commentary on our current public policies. Fortunately, the cliff-hanger ending promises a sequel." *—School Library Journal*

And coming soon:
SPECIALS

PUBLISHED BY SIMON PULSE

WANTED

Single Teen Reader in search of a FUN romantic comedy read!

How Not to Spend Your Senior Year
BY CAMERON DOKEY

Royally Jacked
BY NIKI BURNHAM

Ripped at the Seams
BY NANCY KRULIK

Cupidity
BY CAROLINE GOODE

Spin Control
BY NIKI BURNHAM

South Beach Sizzle
BY SUZANNE WEYN & DIANA GONZALEZ

She's Got the Beat
BY NANCY KRULIK

30 Guys in 30 Days
BY MICOL OSTOW

Animal Attraction
BY JAMIE PONTI

A Novel Idea
BY AIMEE FRIEDMAN

Scary Beautiful
BY NIKI BURNHAM

Getting to Third Date
BY KELLY McCLYMER

Available from Simon Pulse **Published by Simon & Schuster**